CONTINGENCY PLANS FOR THE APOCALYPSE

S.B. Divya is a lover of science, maths and fiction. She is the Nebula Award–nominated author of *Runtime* (2016), and co-editor of the Hugo Award–nominated science-fiction podcast *Escape Pod*, with Mur Lafferty (2018). Her short stories have been published in various magazines, including *Analog, Uncanny* and Tor.com, and her writing also appears in the indie game *Rogue Wizards*. She holds degrees in computational neuroscience and signal processing, and she worked for twenty years as an electrical engineer before becoming an author. She enjoys subverting expectations and breaking stereotypes whenever she can.

D1270011

CONTINGENCY PLANS FOR THE APOCALYPSE

AND OTHER POSSIBLE SITUATIONS

S.B. DIVYA

hachette
INDIA

First published in 2019 by Hachette India
(Registered name: Hachette Book Publishing India Pvt. Ltd)
An Hachette UK company
www.hachetteindia.com

1

Copyright © 2019 S.B. Divya

See p. 253 for the publication history of the stories in this volume.

S.B. Divya asserts the moral right to be identified as
the author of this work.

This is a work of fiction. Any resemblance to real persons, living or dead, or
actual events or locales is purely coincidental.

ISBN 978-93-88322-43-0

For sale in the Indian Subcontinent only

Hachette Book Publishing India Pvt. Ltd
4th & 5th Floors, Corporate Centre,
Plot No. 94, Sector 44, Gurugram 122003, India

Typeset in Adobe Jenson Pro 12/15.5
by R Ajith Kumar, New Delhi

Printed and bound in India
by Manipal Technologies Limited, Manipal

To Mrs Bos, my eighth-grade English teacher, for first putting me on the path to writing stories

Nothing's hopeless except never trying.

— C.J. CHERRYH

There is no real ending. It's just the place where you stop the story.

— FRANK HERBERT

CONTENTS

CONTENTS

LOSS OF SIGNAL

When the doors drifted open like wings, when I trained my cameras to the star-flecked blackness, when the metal arms released me from their embrace: that was the moment my first dream came true.

I checked it off the list.

'You're clear of the shuttle, Toby. Begin translunar injection.'

Mission Control's voice sounded in my ear, but I had no ear. I had adapted to that change early on.

'Roger that, Houston.' I'd always wanted to say that. I'd learned how to turn my thoughts into a stream of text, the only form of speech I had. 'Activating ignition for translunar injection.'

The engines roared, but you can't feel vibrations without bones. You can't yield to acceleration without flesh.

'Thirty seconds left on the burn, Houston.'

'Trajectory change is looking good from here.'

I switched off the engines with a thought command. 'Delta-v is on target, Houston. I'm on my way to the moon.'

A burst of applause, then: 'Safe travels, Toby. Let's make history together!'

After that I coasted in silence for several hours. My cylindrical housing turned slowly, like a rotisserie, so it wouldn't overheat. The Earth rose in my visual field, filling it with her iconic, marbled glory – half in jewelled light, half in deepest shadow.

Checked off another one.

The sensation of cold built during the quiet, darker intervals. I shouldn't have felt anything so corporeal. I hadn't for years, not since the phantom pains of lost limbs and absent organs. They'd wired me for sight and hearing. I didn't miss the rest.

———

When your dreams are fuelled by words and pictures, when your body has you trapped in one position and you want so badly to do great things: that's when you memorize all those famous lines. You act out the scenes in your head, and you're always the hero.

Heroes aren't bothered by the cold. They don't complain. My mother never did. She would come home at night and rub bag balm on to her hands. Chapped skin would curl away, powder white against coffee black, especially after she'd pulled a double dishwashing shift.

On one of those nights, years ago, I asked her, 'Does it hurt?'

'Like the devil on Sunday, baby, but it's only pain. Buckle down and push through. Get the job done.'

———

She told me that a lot, those first few months after the transfer. My old body was worthless, but my brain was good. The engineers tossed around words I looked up later. *Plasticity, neurogenesis, connectomics.* Bottom line: the dying, wheelchair-bound sixteen-year-old could make history in the space programme. Sign me up!

But the change was hard, often painful. My new home lacked the usual body parts. I was as frustrated as ever, though I was alive.

'You're lucky to be here, son,' Mama scolded. 'Getting a second chance like this. I don't want to hear you fussing.'

———

Pain was my worst friend even before the transfer. You think you'd get used to it after a while – that failing nerves would mean numbness – but bodies don't work that way. They take time to die. They make you pay while you wait.

Sometimes Mama couldn't afford the co-pay for my meds. Sometimes I went days without pain medication while we waited for the pharmacy to reach the doctor, because the government thought Mama might be dealing drugs. As if she had time for that.

———

I tried to ignore the phantom chill of space. I could handle the discomfort – I'd been through worse in my old body – but the sensation disturbed me. I slept, my only escape.

'Toby, this is Houston with a signal check.'

I woke.

'I hear you loud and clear, Houston.'

'We've uploaded the latest numbers for your lunar orbit insertion. Engine readouts look good. How are things at your end?'

Text can't betray chattering teeth. Not that I had any, but that's how cold I felt. I wanted my mother's warm bulk against me. We'd shared a bed long past the age when kids and parents typically stop, but needing someone to roll you over at night isn't typical.

'Houston, I'd like to talk to my mother.'

Is it wrong for a nineteen-year-old man – if you could still call me a man – to ask for his mama?

'We can patch her in.'

After a few minutes, she spoke. 'I'm here. What's the matter, baby?'

'I'm really cold. Freezing. It's hard to think.'

The seconds stretched like tiny eternities. Do we ever lose the fear of disappointing our mothers?

'Toby, this is Doctor Keil. Does the sensation decrease with auditory input?'

'Some.'

'What about visual?'

'Maybe? There isn't much to see at the moment.'

'I suspect it's an artefact of sensory deprivation.'

My mother and I had looked up those words long ago. The past two years had been free of phantoms. I'd been able to train with NASA in comfort. Why would they come back now?

Nobody likes surprises in space travel.

'How about I read to you?' Mama suggested. 'All those books you tried to share with me... I never had the time before, but I do now.'

'Sure. Let's try that.'

With my mother's voice in my ears, I captained a vast starship. I battled dragons; teleported across the galaxy; invoked strange and powerful spells. I had superhuman strength and extrasensory perception.

Mama read aloud from books whose spines had been white with use when I'd bought them. That she hadn't sold them came as a surprise. She kept on until her voice got scratchy, and then Fred Shu over at mission control took a shift, and then others. Mama's voice kept the cold at bay better than anyone else's.

'Folks, I hate to interrupt, but we have ten minutes to the loss of signal point. We need Toby to run a systems check.'

Was I that close to the moon already? Indeed, her alabaster curve swept into my peripheral vision.

'All readouts are green, Houston.'

'What about you, Toby? How are you doing?'

'I'm scared.'

The thought slipped to text by accident. It happens sometimes when I'm not careful.

A long pause before the reply came: 'We don't have any

good ideas here, I'm sorry to say. You'll have ten minutes of radio silence before the burn, and then another twenty after. Can you handle it?'

I muted the transmitter to keep my thoughts safe.

'Toby, if it's too painful to execute the lunar orbit insertion, stay passive and let the moon's gravity shoot you back. That's why we chose this trajectory. It's better than a misfire. Do you copy?'

Unmute. 'Copy that, Houston.'

What they didn't say: give up on circumnavigating the moon. Fail to prove that humanity doesn't need bodies to crew its spacecraft; that we don't have to wait for artificial intelligences; that kids like me can go where few able-bodied adults have been...and beyond.

If I couldn't survive the dark silence, the loneliness, I would set the test program back by years. The Apollo missions had crews. The astronauts kept company, cracked wise, backed each other up. My kind would be alone in the dark. The world was watching, waiting. If I gave up, what were the odds they'd give us a second chance?

'You can do it, baby. It's only thirty minutes of quiet, and Mama's going to be right here when you come back.'

She spoke as if I were a child. I hated that, normally. Now? I wanted to cry.

But you can't make tears without ducts and glands. You can't sob without lungs.

I transmitted: 'I'll do my best.'

'One minute to LOS.'

The moon loomed, familiar and white, filling most of my

view as I rotated toward it: my cratered dream; my harsh mistress. The blanched horizon terrified me.

'Baby, you do what you need to and come back safe. You've made enough history.'

'Five seconds to LOS.'

The last thing I heard was Mama's voice: 'I love you, baby, no matter what.'

Silence deafens. Cold burns.

How do we make sense of such oxymorons? Insanity, that's how. If someone offers you a chance to cheat death the sane response is to accept it, right?

Maybe not.

My mind had played all kinds of tricks on me, but the cold of space was the cruellest. Chill seeped into bones I didn't have. Non-existent fingers and toes ached, like they had on winter nights without gas. I shivered without muscles.

Ten minutes to decide: be a hero, or go to sleep? Jim Lovell, Sally Ride, Guy Bluford. What would Toby Benson mean to history?

I could use my 'free return' to Earth. I could sleep and let gravity do its work. I could see the headlines: *Toby Benson, Man–Machine Hybrid, Fails to Replicate Apollo 8 Mission.*

Better to use my imagination – my strongest remaining asset. I was Amundsen at the South Pole; Shackleton trapped by ice. I had to persist or doom my crew to death.

No second chances. No excuses. No sleep.

The Sandman had often carried me away when I was a child. In his dreaming embrace, I'd found solace. Sleep would swaddle me like a cosy blanket. I never wanted to leave it, especially on school mornings.

'I'm still tired, Mama,' I would protest.

'Get up, Toby! I'm working twelve-hour shifts, and you're telling me you're tired? I don't think so.'

During winter, ice coated the half-dozen steps from our tenement door to the sidewalk.

'Clumsy,' Mama chided the first time I slipped. 'Watch yourself! I can't be paying for broken bones.'

Each year I fell more often. Fell down. Fell off. Fell asleep. My sixth-grade teacher convinced Mama to take me to a doctor. A year passed before we got a diagnosis, but I looked up a lot of words in those twelve months: ataxia, dysarthria, cardiomyopathy, trans-synaptic atrophy.

I did all the reading. Mama heard the executive summary: my nerves were failing. My muscles weren't working right, and they were going to get worse until they stopped.

The heart is a muscle. Mama hadn't known that.

———

Once upon a time, I was Toby, age fourteen, living in Chicago. I lay on the sidewalk, unable to move. For hours I watched snowflakes drift from the night sky, clouds obscuring the stars, the tiny crystals taking their places.

People walked right past me. I knew what they were thinking: another loser kid, high on drugs, not worth helping.

If our landlady hadn't recognized me on her way home... Well, you know how those stories end.

———

An orange light flashed: one minute before I had to start the burn. If I stayed passive, the moon would slingshot me back to Earth. If the cold distracted me while I worked the engines, I could drift for eternity or crash into the lunar surface.

I was alone again, this time on the quiet side of the moon. No one would help. No one would see.

Frost buzzed through me like a swarm of bees, stinging my body in a million places. You can't breathe through pain if you have no lungs. You can't run warm-up laps without legs. You can't huddle up when you're all alone.

But I wasn't helpless. I was a rocket. I had engines. My new body thrummed with latent power.

Time to write a new story.

When the countdown reached zero, I sent the thought to activate ignition. I applied the right amount of energy, the exact direction of thrust. I gritted my imaginary teeth and triple-checked the readouts as my velocity changed. Then I turned off the engines.

The moon's gravity held me in stable orbit for as long as I desired. Craters dusted in abalone whites and greys filled my view in one direction. I watched the familiar contours pass by – Secchi, Mount Marilyn, the Sea of Tranquillity – their names etched in my memory better than my own face. On my other side, the stars sang their vast, maddening, frigid aria, but

I was safe in a lunar embrace. Safe enough to let myself sleep. Blissful oblivion took me for the next twenty minutes.

———

When the sun's light warmed me again; when a cacophony of cheers filled my hearing; when my planet rose like a robin's egg from a shadowed nest: then, I checked off one more item.

CONTINGENCY PLANS FOR
THE APOCALYPSE

My apocalypse doesn't ride on horseback or raise the dead or add suns to the sky. It arrives by tank and drone, the strict report of automatic weapons, the spying eyes of neighbours. It seeks my spouse's life. Mine, too. I don't expect to survive.

Chula has better odds. She is a four-time triathlete, perfect eyesight, no injuries. She can lift our six-year-old the way I haul a fire log. If anyone can outrun the law, it's Chula.

'When they come for us,' I said, after Kaila was born, 'you take the children and the backpack, and head for the safe house.'

Chula's blue eyes narrowed. 'And you'll catch up. You have a pack, too. We'll go side by side, like always.'

'Sure. If I'm alive.'

Her glare could melt Antarctica. 'And what if I'm dead instead of you?'

'That's so much less likely. I wouldn't plan on it.'

She raised her pale brows to emphasize my hypocrisy, but I didn't care. If our survival depended on me, we were in trouble.

———

Like any ordinary evening, I put the baby down in our room after feeding her. Night darkens the sky. We leave the lights off as much as possible to avoid surveillance from the outside. I trip over the corner of the dining room rug, the one that's bent upward from all the other times my foot caught it. (My muscles are clumsy thanks to the polio redux pandemic, but I've had lots of practice at falling; I know how to avoid sprains and broken bones.) I land on my forearms, nearly prone.

A bullet sings over my head and penetrates Chula's.

For five seconds, I freeze.

For five seconds, I stop breathing.

My mind refuses to accept the image in front of me. *No. No. No no no.*

The inhale comes in a rush.

I move.

Her neck has no pulse.

I fling a blanket over my beloved's body and cover it all: the blond hair now matted with blood, the shards of glass catching the streetlight, the limbs splayed like a sleeping toddler's, the stain spreading outward on that rug – that thrice-damned rug, which I will never see again.

A yellow thread snags on the hinge of my wrist prosthesis. Chula's favourite colour. I yank it out and stuff it into the centre of my bra as I crawl across the room. More bullets trash our windows. A rubber band made of devastation tightens around my heart and lungs.

I speak my farewell in my thoughts. To say it aloud is to provide evidence to the sensors. I wish I had time to give Chula a farewell kiss. I wish she'd lived. I hope the people outside think we're both dead.

In the windowless hall, I stand and run. My booted feet slam against hickory planks, our home improvement project from back before fear decorated our lives. Now, we sleep in our clothes and wear shoes in the house. Photos flash by along the beige wall, memories outlined in black, all but the newest: the four of us huddled in bed after I gave birth to Kaila. That one I taped up, unframed. It gives easily and fits in the back pocket of my jeans.

I burst into our room and reach under the antique bedframe. I pull out my backpack, filled to eighteen pounds, the same weight I carried across the Andes during our Choquequirao trek. I was a decade younger and fitter then, but today I have to travel only one-fourth the distance. At sea level, that's manageable. It has to be.

I tighten the straps on the pack. The baby sling hangs on one corner of the crib. Kaila whimpers as I snug her swaddled form against my torso. I lock my arm into a static, supportive position under her, and turn it off to conserve battery.

In the adjacent bedroom, Myles hides under his bed like we have taught him to. His dark curls catch the last light from the window. He has the same hair as his father, killed a year ago while attempting to cross the border, the very same one we're headed for.

'Time to go, baby,' I whisper.

He crawls out. 'Where's Chula?'

I'd failed to rehearse the words for this question because I didn't expect to be here. 'I'll explain later.'

Suspicion darkens his six-year-old face, sets his jaw. *Not a tantrum, not now, baby, please, we gotta go.*

'Don't forget Dino,' I say.

It's part distraction, part truth, but it works. Myles lunges for the stuffed Tyrannosaurus rex and clasps it to his chest. We run to the side door and out into the chill night – oh, I forgot the jackets, did we pack jackets? – but we can't turn back because the tank turret looms above the fourth house down the street. A white cover hides the surgical van beside the house. I don't dare use it, not with all that damning evidence inside, but I send it a silent farewell. Another tie to Chula, severed.

We duck through the hidden door in the back fence, down the alley, across a demented mosaic of chipped stone and glass. I grab my phone and increase the light amplification in my implanted lenses. (They told me it's an experimental technology with some risks. I told them to shut up and take my money.) I follow the snaking line of garden hose that surrounds a data cable, poached for my illegal purposes.

The hose runs into a plain door set into a low building. I pull it free and fling it back towards the house. They can't know where we went. My thumb goes against the sensor-lock. A light next to it blinks red. I curse under my breath and lick my too-dry skin and try again. *Turn green, turn green, turn green – yes!*

I open the door. *Where is Myles? He was just here. How could he – oh shit!*

Flames engulf our house and balloon outward. The light blows my vision and all I see is a little shadow flying through the air, away from the back fence, toward me. Myles lands head-first.

A second rubber band, made of recrimination, constricts my heart and lungs. I run to my son, wrap my arm around his chest, and drag him through the door. I lay him down. Be alive, please baby, be alive. His chest rises and falls. Relief swims in dizzy circles around me.

Dim red lights wake at our presence. Racks of servers line the walls. Bundles of cables stretch across the ceiling to a staircase dug through rock and earth. Our escape route normally ferries large quantities of data and the occasional service person.

I peer into the gloom. I can't carry them both downstairs. *Goddammit, Chula, you should be here!*

I trip as I come off the last step and land on my knees rather than my newborn. Kaila fusses when I place her on the ground next to the backpack, but she doesn't raise a cry. I limp my way up to retrieve Myles, unlocking my prosthesis and powering it on as I climb.

Once I have them both at the bottom, I allow myself a minute to breathe and listen. No sound penetrates from outside. No door slams open above us. No one shouts. I pull the kill switch in the wall – our little modification. Dirt seals off the room above. The stairs end in nothing.

We're in a tunnel lined with network access. I'd patch

into a cable if I could, but it's all useless now. Instead, I grab my phone, which is nearly out of battery. We have a system across the family, a handful of sites where we leave nonsense text, meaningful only to one another. I write: *Had to visit the loo. With the T. rex and the raptor. Lost my other ring.* I scan all the locations. My brother hasn't left a message in over a week. My parents and Chula's live in friendly states, thank goodness. Two less things to worry about.

Myles whimpers. In the glow from the screen, I see patches of crimson across my boy's skin. The soles of his shoes are melted – to his feet? I shudder and banish the thought. He's breathing. He's alive. He'll be fine. He will, he has to be.

The tunnel shivers around us. Dust motes dance in the artificial light. I shove the phone into my pocket. We can't linger too long. I consider the pack, sized for multi-day hikes. Myles is small for his age. *Maybe.* Out come the spare clothes, a multi-tool, a sticker book, hiking poles, diapers, formula, snack bars, water bottles, an optical cube with all our memories. The jackets must have been in Chula's pack.

I use the knife from the tool to tear holes on either side of the pack's bottom, then I slide Myles in and snug the compressor straps around him. In the outer pouches, I cram in six diapers – they're lightweight – a spare outfit for Kaila, three packets of formula, two snack bars, one water bottle, and the data cube. It's an old dilemma: weight versus comfort.

The multi-tool goes in my back pocket, my only weapon, should I need one. The baby goes on my front. My son rides on my back, a forty-four-pound load. His head lolls against my shoulder. In the interest of minimizing weight, I remove my prosthesis and add it to the discards on the ground.

The hiking pole helps with my new centre of gravity. Grief and determination fuel my steps. If I don't survive, neither do they.

———

Chula strides through the tunnel, Myles running alongside. I imagine him whining that his legs are tired. Chula tucks him under an arm, her bicep bulging but not strained. In this vision, I'm a ghost floating behind them. All goes according to plan, and they escape. Loss and pain are not mine to bear. I don't have to be the strong one.

———

For twelve hours, I walk. Trudge. Plod. Stumble. Every three hours, I stop to feed Kaila, half from my breasts, half formula, all of it while standing or kneeling. The yellow thread tucked into my bra draws my gaze as often as my baby's dark eyes. I reach my right hand back to check Myles's pulse and breathing. I slide water into his searing mouth with my fingertips and hope he doesn't dehydrate too much.

The things I can manage to think about are time, quantities and steps. Others, I push away – my inevitable failure, Chula sprawled on the rug, our cold, stiff bodies lying in this catacomb-like space.

Should we have stayed in this state? We asked the question at least once a week. I found the patients and guided the van.

Chula and the robots performed the abortions. In this place, our life-saving service was punishable by death. We knew the risk. We couldn't lie to ourselves about that.

But it wasn't supposed to be me, here, dragging our family to safety.

Chula contacted the resistance, made the arrangements. (We kept my identity secret to better protect the children, whom I carried, for the same reason.) She had the reputation: a doctor, one with a rare skill. I was a data miner. Nothing special about that.

At last, a staircase rises ahead. The cables converge upward. My legs weigh more than elephants. Damn elephants. Why do they have to be so massive? Step, step, one…more…step.

I'm through the door into another data centre, equally unattended. My phone is dead, but I remember the route to the safe house. I remember most of what I see, a leftover habit from years of wearing glasses (and being nearly blind without them). Dawn glows in the eastern sky. It lights our way to a low, sprawling house painted grey with white trim. The side door has an electronic lock. I enter the eight-digit code. A faint click indicates that it works.

I stumble inside. A couple emerges from a bedroom. Their alarmed expressions tell me everything about our appearance. A question buzzes through my ears into my head.

'Chula Smith.' I whisper her name as an incantation and sway on the tiled floor, surrounded by walls and furniture and warmth. We're safe, for now.

———

They leave us in a bedroom decorated with faded posters of augmented-reality stars. They remind me of my past life – trawling the Net for good data, piecing it together like clues in a mystery. The skill came in handy for finding those in need of Chula's services. Most people don't notice the breadcrumb trails they leave on the Internet.

Myles lies on the single bed, his burns dressed as best as we could, half a bowl of chicken broth coaxed in by small spoonfuls. Kaila and I rest on the floor. An unzipped sleeping bag lies beneath us. My heart, entrapped by its two rubber bands, beats with the restless fury of a butterfly in a net.

Outside our door, our hosts' voices rise in argument. They gave me code names – Bravo and Foxtrot – and didn't ask for mine, but they know I'm not Chula.

'Smith is the priority evacuee, not the family,' says Foxtrot. 'We can't make an unscheduled supply run without authorization. Two more days. They'll last.'

'She has a four-month-old baby!' Bravo sounds upset. 'And her child needs medical attention, more than we can give.'

'And we need to maintain our cover or we're no good to anybody. I don't like it either, but we can't risk everything for a low-priority group.'

Their voices drop away. They use the wrong pronouns for me, but I'm in no position to correct them.

Bravo's right. Myles needs a doctor. If Chula were here, she could take care of him. If Chula were here, they'd be on their way to the border already. If Chula were here... If, if, if.

Kaila whimpers. I sit up to give her my left breast, the better one. I lean against a wall and use my legs to support her body, but it takes time, and she's crying before I'm ready. She's calmer when we switch sides. Her black eyes stare into mine, all serious business until a smile breaks her suction and lights up her face.

I can't help returning it, but I'm thinking, please make enough milk today, *please for today and tomorrow and the next, until we get out, because we used the last of the formula and it's rationed and these people don't have a baby so we can't get more.*

For twenty minutes after she stops feeding, Kaila is sunshine and roses. When she fusses again, I try to latch her on, but she's having none of it. Her wail brings in our hosts.

'You need to quiet her down,' Bravo says. 'We're not supposed to have children here.'

'She's hungry,' I say. Shame heats my neck and cheeks.

Foxtrot frowns. 'Can't you feed her?'

'I did. I – I can't make enough for her, and I'm out of formula.'

The two of them exchange a look before leaving the room. This time, their conversation doesn't carry. I imagine Foxtrot saying, 'That's one more strike against them. What a useless person. We should send them back to die,' so I force my wobbly, spent leg muscles to stand, and I bounce my baby. My right shoulder aches from her weight, and my ghost arm prickles with pain. I rock Kaila through it all until she gives in and sleeps, and then, at last, so do I.

To my surprise, Foxtrot tells me the next morning to get ready to leave. I don't question it. We sit in the back of an old gasoline-powered truck, manually driven. Myles is stretched out by my feet, and Kaila hangs in the sling. Empty crates fill the remaining space, hiding us in case anyone opens the doors. This couple imports produce from across the border. Who better to smuggle contraband than someone with a legitimate business?

We move through the sparse early-morning traffic on the slow roads, the ones where you can still drive a vehicle yourself. Through the gaps in the wooden slats, I catch glimpses of posters. 'Jesus welcomes all.' 'Life is sacred.' 'A righteous husband will provide.' Sometimes I only see a few words, but I've memorized them. Chula and Myles's father and I had a marriage, but not one that this state would recognize.

'Damn,' Foxtrot says.

The van careens to the right and accelerates. I brace my feet against a crate to keep from sliding.

'What's happening?' I call out. The gap in the cab's rear sliding window lets my voice through.

'Patrol.'

We turn sharp left, and Myles slides to the right. I grab him before his head hits the wall.

'Do you have a mobile? I can route you!'

Foxtrot slides the window further and tosses me a device wrapped in yellow flower-print. Our eyes meet for a second.

'My daughter's.' Foxtrot's words clip.

I launch the map software on a dead girl's phone, unlikely to be traced. If I had my virtual-reality headset, I could work faster. I do what I can manually, fingers flying across the screen. Data overlays stack tiny icons – not my customized versions, but no time for that. I scan for safe zones to hide a truck. A produce warehouse lies three miles out of our way. Bonus: we'd pass under a freeway bridge to get there.

'Two blocks, then left and an immediate right,' I call.

By the time Foxtrot makes the right-hand turn, I'm ready with three more instructions, and so we dance with our pursuers, avoiding known camera sites and drone-zones. This low-bandwidth communication is awkward. I would guide Chula's surgical van remotely, directing the auto-driver from home. I could avoid patrols and prying electronics without speaking a word.

'Hard right at the three-way,' I call.

Our tires screech, and the truck keels, but we keep most of our speed. Foxtrot drives almost as well as an auto-car.

'Second left, through a tunnel, and then right into the driveway and stop!'

And that's it. We wait with the engine off. Blood rushes in my ears to fill the silence. My heart beats so hard that Kaila must feel it through the sling.

Another truck, similar in shape and size to ours, sits next to us. The mobile's data shows a third one parked beyond. The rolling metal door of a warehouse is in front of us, the words 'Farm Fresh With Love' painted in bold green letters across it.

Foxtrot crouches into the wheel-well so that they're not immediately visible from outside. I scrunch down and install my custom overlay. Nothing to do now but wait.

A drone buzzes past, then another, ten minutes later. They blip on the mobile's screen, little white skull icons.

Patience.

The sun rises over the warehouse. For two miles in each direction, the map is clear of skulls and coffins and machine guns (the icons for tanks and foot patrols). I give us another fifteen minutes to be sure. We can't afford much longer, or Kaila will wake for her next feeding before we cross the border. That would end us.

'Let's go,' I say.

Foxtrot sits up and starts the engine. I'm grateful for their trust – that I know what I'm doing.

———

As we approach the border station, I rearrange the crates to block us from all sides. I can't see the squat, hard-edged buildings, but I remember them from pictures, their walls studded with cameras.

The sun blazes over endless desert. The back of the truck becomes an oven as soon as we stop moving. I peek through the crates to see what's happening. The view isn't good.

'Documents.' A deep voice speaks the word.

A hand takes something from Foxtrot, then returns it and says, 'Please exit the vehicle for a security pat down.' Smug. 'And cavity search.'

The truck jostles as Foxtrot exits the cab, out of my view.

Does this happen every time? Is this the cost to move us or a regular part of doing business? A third rubber band snaps into place around my heart and lungs. It's made of rage, and I can't breathe. Heat rushes through me. *Keep your hands off my driver! I will rip your goddamn head off and watch the life pour out. I will –*

Foxtrot climbs into the cab.

'Proceed,' the guard says.

We drive on, past two barbed-wire fences set one hundred yards apart, into California, and safety. The word tastes bitter in my thoughts: what kind of safe place uses people like that to secure its borders? But, on this side at least, the work that Chula and I did would be legal.

If I close my eyes, I see her body sprawled in our house. I see the photo of our spouse's body laid out in the desert, a cruel souvenir sent by the border troops. Am I a coward for running away? Should I go back when Kaila is older? No, whispers Chula's voice. No way, whispers our husband's. Keep the children safe. Raise them. We agreed on that when we decided to stay in Arizona, in a house reduced to rubble, in a life burnt to ash.

———

We stop again in half an hour, just as Kaila is beginning to stir. Through gaps, I see a single-story ranch house with other small buildings behind it. Foxtrot opens the back gate and moves the crates out of our way. I blink in the sudden brightness. Two brown-skinned men pull Myles out on a stretcher and carry him towards the house. I force myself to meet Foxtrot's gaze.

'I'm sorry about the...search,' I say. 'Thank you for helping us.' The most inadequate words I've ever spoken.

Foxtrot nods.

Do you have to go back? The question dies before it reaches my lips. I know the answer because I lived it, too. I risked my family so that we could help the women who couldn't escape. If the state hadn't found us, we'd still be there.

'Take care,' Foxtrot says.

The truck rumbles down a dirt road towards a field lined with vegetables.

I follow my son and discover my mother waiting inside.

'How...?'

'They got word to me as soon as you crossed the border,' she says, 'and I got your message before that. I've been waiting nearby, just in case.'

She opens her arms to me, and I sink into them.

'I'm so sorry about Chula,' she says.

She doesn't say, 'I told you so,' or 'How could you do this to your children?' or any of the dozen other recriminations I've imagined in her voice.

Kaila squirms and fusses, sandwiched between us. I need to feed her. Over my mother's shoulder I see Myles on the bed, his chest rising and falling, his eyelids fluttering. He hasn't woken enough to speak. I wonder what silent price he's paid. Was our work worth the cost of my son's condition, of my spouses' lives? I may never have the answer to that. Maybe none exists.

As I feed my baby, the bands that constricted me loosen, enough for regret and sadness and rage to expand. My tears land on Kaila's chest. For now, it's enough that I got us out. The children are safe and alive. I have no desire to consider what comes next, not yet, not today. Right now, our survival is all that matters.

MICROBIOTA AND THE MASSES

A Love Story

The scents of earth – loam, pollen, compost, the exhalation of leaves – permeated the inside of Moena Sivaram's airtight home. She stood near the southeast corner and misted the novice bromeliads. The epiphytes clutched the trunk of an elephant ear tree, its canopy stretching up to the clear, SmartWindow-paned roof and shading everything below.

Moena whispered to the plants: 'Amma's here, little babies. You're safe with me, but you must grow those roots.' With her isolated life, these would be her only children.

She walked barefoot to the sunny citrus grove in the western side of the house. The soil beneath her feet changed from cool and moist to hard and gritty. eBees buzzed among the flowers. She hummed in harmony, a Carnatic song about love birds that was a century old. The heady perfume of orange and lime blossoms filled her up and made her blood sing along. This was home; this, and not the traditional jasmine and rose gardens of Bangalore; this, where her eyes didn't water nor her nose itch.

Diffuse sunlight shone through the SmartWindows panelling the walls. One rectangle stuck out like a cloudy diamond in an otherwise glittering pendant. Moena pulled her tablet from her pocket, brought up the diagnostic software. Red letters delivered bad news: faults in the air and light filters.

The latter mattered little. The plants would get enough sun from the functional panes. The former, though, meant that outside air had infiltrated the house.

Moena's throat closed. Her heart raced. *Stay calm!* But her hands wouldn't listen, clutching each other, fingers twisting like vines around branches. She couldn't breathe! All those microbes: she imagined them invading her sanctum, those wriggly, single-celled prokaryotes.

She shuddered, dropped to the ground, lay prone. Her cheek touched beloved dirt. Safe dirt. *Inhale! Exhale! Again!* She tilted her face, lowered her tongue, and licked. The potent esters of her domestic biome worked their magic, taking over the hamster-wheels in her brain and applying the brakes.

Her hands unclenched. Shoulder blades fell back. Heart slowed. *Stupid brain. We can deal with this.*

The eBees agreed. 'Yes, yes, yes,' they sang.

Moena went to her supply closet. The air-filter mask inside looked like an insectoid alien: tinted plastic across the eyes, and three jutting cylinders over the mouth and nose areas. Moena pulled it on. The clean air lacked the comforting odours of home, but at least she was protected.

She sealed the offending window pane with heavy plastic and duct tape, then rolled the sensor cart over. *Good!* All air now flowed from the inside out, as it should. She sent a message to SmartWindows Incorporated, requesting a repair person and marking the issue urgent.

———

Rahul the repairman arrived looking like Moena's favourite porn star: faded jeans, tight white T-shirt, cinnamon-bark skin, boyish black curls. She admired the image on her tablet, fed from the door camera. Too bad she couldn't touch him. Her face flushed. The space between her legs tightened. *Not now, and not him, idiot body.* Not any man or woman infested with outside microbiota.

She slapped her cheeks lightly and blew out a hot breath. Syed – her outside man – was away at his second cousin's wedding in Mysore. She would have to deal with Rahul herself.

'Please wait there,' she said, a delayed audio reply to his intercom buzz.

Moena opened the supply closet and grimaced at the grey isolation suit hanging in the back. It reeked of industrial plastic and factory esters. She grabbed a handful of soil from the floor and sprinkled it into the suit. Then she pulled it and the air mask on.

She stepped into the airlocked foyer, clinched the inner door seals, and walked out the front. To his credit, Rahul only took a half-step back. His dark eyes widened like a bud opening to rain. Questions sprouted and withered on his lips – parted to show endearingly crooked teeth – until he said, 'Miss... Sivaram?'

'Yes. Follow me, please,' Moena said.

She led him across the weedy, barren dirt of her lot. They walked around the thick clay walls of the house to arrive at the faulty SmartWindow. Rahul attached his computer to it via a long cable, vine-like but for its grey colour. He sat on the dirt and began typing.

'The light and air filters are set to opposite extremes,' he said. He spoke English in the well-rounded tones of an educated, middle-class Indian. 'Most people use these windows to reduce the ultraviolet while permitting air circulation into the house.'

I am not most people. Out loud: 'You don't talk like a repairman.'

Rahul smiled. 'I'm an F.A.E. – a field applications engineer. We repair but we also have technical backgrounds.' He paused, squinted up at her. 'Tell me, are you *the* Moena Sivaram?'

Tendrils of anxiety coiled in Moena's stomach. The plane crash that killed her parents had been well publicized, but the story had faded from the news years ago. Why would this man jab her with a question about it?

'I am.'

'Your thesis on fresh water bioremediation was incredible. How come you haven't published any papers since then?'

Moena gaped behind the mask. 'Just who are you?'

'Sorry, I should have explained. I'm a volunteer with Hariharan Ecological Group. They've taken your design and used it to treat local water pollution. It's been a great success. You're famous among us. I thought, perhaps, you might be running a laboratory in the house, what with these window settings.'

Moena reeled at the orthogonality of the question and stared at her reflection in the SmartWindow. Her suit resembled the spent husk of a chrysalis. If only she could emerge a gorgeous butterfly, she could stun Rahul into silence as well.

'I am conducting experiments in the house,' she admitted. 'I wear this suit to keep the environment as isolated as I can.'

'Could I – I mean, if it's not too much trouble – could I see what you're doing?'

Moena shook her head like a leaf frenzied by the wind. Rahul...inside her house? Inside her? Possibilities tumbled in her mind, gorgeous and terrifying. *Impossible!*

'No, of course not.' He turned back to his computer. 'Sorry for asking.'

Moena reached out to him, drew her hand back. She had no right to his body.

The afternoon sun blazed from high in the summer sky as the silence stretched. Heat built inside Moena's isolation suit. Her shirt clung to her torso. Rivulets of sweat trickled down her neck and collected at the waistband of her shorts. She sat still, channelling the *atman* of a tree stump.

'Aha!' Rahul said at last.

The window cleared to perfect transparency. Rahul reinstalled it and stowed his computer. He handed her a memory cube.

'You'll want to update all of the windows with this version of software. The problem is that your filter settings are below virus size. The old software kept getting stuck in an interrupt routine and eventually hanging. This version should prevent that from happening.'

'Thank you,' Moena said. Part of her wished every window would fail, once a week, so Rahul would come again.

'The company will bill you directly. Best of luck with the research.'

Moena nodded. The mask bobbled. Rahul walked out of the front gate, latching it closed behind him. She was alone.

The sterilization wash in her foyer had never felt so tedious. Once she was fully inside, Moena yanked off the mask and took several deep, relieving breaths. She peeled away the sweaty suit, let it crumple to the floor.

Soil wormed into the gaps between her bare toes. Leaves and fronds brushed her hands as she walked – nearly ran – to her bedroom. It looked much as it had when her parents were alive: a single bed, a narrow wardrobe painted yellow, a matching desk with shelves above it. The coffin was the exception.

The adult-sized container lay between the bed and the room's boarded-up window. The device's actual name was 'Virtual Reality Recumbent Booth', but the world had decided that was too unwieldy. Moena agreed.

She browsed the preset visuals under 'male'. This one had beetle brows. That one was too pale. Dozens had overlays with blue eyes and blond hair. She stopped at a face that was close enough to Rahul's. The hair needed more curl and the eyes wanted to be smaller, but she could adjust those when her body wasn't pulsing with need.

The coffin's interior walls cosied up to her, running its – *his* – hands over her body, blowing warm breath against her neck, pressing itself – *himself!* – into her empty spaces.

Tension wanted release, but Moena's mind refused to fall into the illusion. She cut the session short.

What would a lover feel like, for real? She shivered. *Think of the microflora! The exchange of so much more than fluid.* And where would it happen? Here, in her bed? In the sanctum of her home? The biome would be corrupted, and her hard work set back by years. *Idiot! Forget him!*

———

But Rahul persisted in her thoughts, like a splinter that wormed deeper the more she tried to pry it out. Moena called the only friend left from her outside days: her fellow graduate student, now Professor Das.

Ananya's broad brown face appeared on the tablet screen accompanied by the clamour of children.

'Let me get somewhere quiet.'

'You have to save me,' Moena said, after her friend relocated.

Ananya cocked an eyebrow. 'Do you need some new cultures?'

'No. Bacteria can't help me. I've been infected by a man, a glorious specimen of male *Homo sapiens!*'

'Infected? What? Did you have sex with someone?'

Moena laughed at her friend's horrified expression. 'No. I haven't touched him. Mmmmm…but I want to. Am I selfish for staying in here? For using my research to benefit myself and not the world?'

'What? Mo, you're not making any sense. Are you okay? How's your biome?'

'The verdant lovelies are fine. Creepy crawlies and microbiota are good. My blood results came back in normal ranges last month. But my heart – my heart is parched for company! He said I'm famous. They're using my thesis. Should I be out there, helping? Fighting the good fight?'

'First: you're not selfish for keeping yourself from chronic illness. Second: you are brilliant, and you should be publishing your results. Third: who is this chap and how has he gotten under your skin?'

'His name is Rahul. Window repairman and eco-warrior supreme, with skin like creamy cocoa-butter.'

Her friend rolled her eyes. 'Get a grip. You haven't touched another human being in over five years. You want to risk everything for him?' Her expression softened. 'If you get sick again, you'll have to give him up.'

'Bridges, crossings, et cetera, dear Professor. Besides, I can't be myself with him so this love affair won't last. Short, torrid, over!'

'What do you mean?'

'He won't want to date Moena Sivaram, wealthy eccentric and victim of tragic circumstance. I'll have to invent a mundane secret identity, someone matched to his station in life.'

'A lie isn't a good foundation for love.'

'I'll keep it to romance, not love. Then can I have your blessing?'

'No. Yes. I don't know,' Ananya sputtered. 'Just…check in with me, okay? I'm worried about you.'

Moena agreed and ended the call. Her fingers approached the keyboard, then curled away, like the leaves of a *Mimosa pudica*: touch-me-not. Her mother's words from a decade ago haunted her.

'When you're of age, Moena, we'll find you a nice boy to marry. Or you'll find one on your own, but keep this in mind: men desire women who can stand up to them and still remain short. They don't want women who are smarter or wealthier or more famous. Better that you forget boys and marriage until you have your own measure.'

Smarter. Wealthier. More famous. Rahul lacked a doctorate. Rahul worked for a living. Rahul's name had never scorched news headlines.

Moena invented a fitting girl for Rahul to love. Meena Sivaraman (close enough that Moena would answer to it): middle class, moderately educated, modestly dressed. A proper, earnest, *sane* young woman with a black braid and a bindi.

Breath came easy. Fingers pattered on the keyboard. Two days later, 'Meena' had a coffee-shop date with Rahul to discuss volunteer opportunities.

———

On the day of their meeting, Moena rejected three different outfits: a traditional sari (too stuffy), a salwar–kameez from a distant aunt (too gaudy), and a dress from her university days in London (too Western). Clad in jeans and a short-sleeved cotton kurti, she stepped out of the house.

She wasn't sure whose eyes were wider, hers or Syed's, as she bolted into the back seat of the car.

'Are you sure, madam?' he asked for the tenth time, peering at her from the driver's seat.

Heart racing, palms sweating, and breath shallow, she said, 'Yes. Drive, please.'

They drove down tree-lined streets, past sky-scraping beehives of apartments and claustrophobic rows of shops. The car's fan was set to recirculate, but the scents of Bangalore crept in through imperfect seals. Moena's throat closed. She gripped the sprigs of holy basil she had brought, crushing the tender leaves. They released a pungent, soothing aroma. She plucked two of them and pressed them into her nostrils. *Better.*

The car lurched to the right, came up to the curb, and stopped.

'This is the place,' Syed said. 'But we can go home, madam. Your health is more important than anything.'

'Thank you, Syed. I'll be okay. I promise I'll call you if I'm not.'

Moena stepped out and drew her first breath of raw city air in five years. Dust assailed her nostrils, drying the tiny hairs and making her sneeze. Rumbling diesel trucks spewed black exhaust. A current of decaying refuse and putrid sewage ran through it all. She gagged.

Bodies moved past her along the uneven slabs of the sidewalk. They stank of hot oil, sweat, sandalwood, fish, jasmine, sex. A stray dog trotted from a cluster of trash to a half-eaten banana. A fly fizzed into Moena's ear, tickling it before moving on.

How did anyone live like this? How had she, for the first twenty-three years of her life? She could almost sense the effluvia penetrating her lungs, polluting her bloodstream. She forced herself to inhale a second time. *Stand straight!* Shoulders back, chin high, hands unclenched: *face the city like everyone else.*

Advertisements plastered the low cinderblock wall to her right, their poster colours faded by rain, their edges frayed and torn. On the other side, gulmohar trees bordered the courtyard, shading the café patrons within. She scanned the crowd. Where was Rahul?

Moena threaded her way between the tables, careful not to touch any thing or person or plant. She spotted Rahul's curly hair and white T-shirt (did he wear nothing else?) in the back corner, at a table sprinkled with pollen from the blossoms above. She pinched her nose against a sneeze.

'Rahul Madhavan?' She tried to sound as if she'd never seen him before.

'Yes. You must be Meena. Please, sit. Shall I order you some coffee?'

Moena swallowed repulsion – non-homemade coffee! – and forced a smile. 'Thanks.'

'You'd like to volunteer for H.E.G. and do some ecological work, yes? Let me tell you about what we do.'

Rahul entered a fifteen-minute monologue with words that felt as much like home as the scent of damp humus. He spoke of water pollution, remediation, plant and bacterial seeding; of community effort and citizen science; of working with the earth and not against it. His hands moved in organic shapes – no sharp edges – and his fingertips came together and burst apart like a ripe seedpod.

Moena watched, listened, sneezed. She swiped at her drippy nostrils with a bleached white handkerchief and sneezed again. Nodded. Smiled. Sneezed. Her coffee arrived and cooled. It stayed untouched, but so did his.

'How does that sound? Like something you can commit to?'

'Absolutely. Once a week. No problem.'

Problems tangled her thoughts faster than she could prune them away.

'Great! I'll send you the information for next week's action.'

'Why aren't you a biologist?'

'Sorry?'

You're not supposed to know that! 'I mean, why are you a volunteer and not working for H.E.G.? You seem so knowledgeable about this.'

'I'm too old?' He flashed his crooked smile. 'I already had an engineering degree when I got interested in remediation. I'm over thirty now. I can't possibly compete in entrance exams. What about you? What brought you to this?'

'I have...a friend. She was sick for a long time, and some of that was because of our water and air. I want to do something for her – for everyone – to improve that.'

'Wonderful! Then I'll see you next week.'

He held out his hand.

Shake it! Moena thrust out her own, let him wrap his fingers around hers. His palm felt warm and smooth, like eucalyptus bark in sunlight. The thrill of contact travelled through her arm and spread, tingling, throughout the rest of her body. *All of him, now!* Her heart raced, mouth dried. Desire gathered force, whipping from a zephyr to a tornado. Her cheeks flushed. Could he tell? Did he sense her tumult?

Rahul let go.

They exited the café together.

Syed picked her up.

The ride home dragged on, an interminable torture of snarled traffic, gaunt beggars, and enough rain to streak the dusty windows.

———

Moena met Rahul and the handful of other volunteers at an oblong lake situated southeast of the city. She felt naked without her isolation suit as she approached the slime-ridden banks.

Bone-white tree trunks dotted the waterline. A quarter kilometre to the left, a rusting hulk of metal heaved a piston up and down. The thrum of its motor drowned the buzzing clouds of insects.

A wave of fetid air blew across Moena. She stumbled back, knelt, and heaved her lunch into a cluster of spindly bushes.

'Sorry. I should have warned you.' Rahul stood next to her. He held out a sky-blue paper mask. 'Wear this. It's coated with menthol.'

Moena accepted it with shaking hands. The astringent scent choked her, squeezing tears from the corners of her eyes, but her stomach settled.

'What is this place?'

'Agara Lake,' Rahul said. 'Rife with industrial metals, plastics, and animal waste.'

Moena stood and caressed a leaf. The bush was a fledgling neem tree, spotted with brown, yellow, and black.

'Poor thing,' she whispered. 'You need help.'

Rahul's pupils dilated. His brow quirked.

Moena shrugged. 'I've always felt more comfortable with plants than people.'

Sunlight glinted, turning Rahul's irises to honey brown. 'Me, too.'

He guided her to the lakeside, his hand light against the small of her back, intimate and yet not.

The volunteers worked in separate domains. Moena's assignment was simple: to collect soil and water samples for analysis.

White foam floated in Rorschach blotches on the surface of the water. Centimetre-high waves lapped at yellowish brown mud. A dead fish bulged at the surface a few metres in.

Guilt constricted her chest with weedy roots. Isolation had restored her health, but at what cost? When had the state of the world become so rotten?

Moena pinched a test tube between thumb and forefinger as if it were a wriggling insect.

Gloves. Boots. Rubber coveralls. All were standard issue protection they'd used in graduate school, but ecological vigilantes – especially here in India – had no such resources. *Do it! Dip your hand in!*

She inched into the lake. Its lukewarm water soaked through her shoes and socks and up along her pants. Moena swallowed a sob. She rooted herself and leaned down. Muscles trembled. *Reach in!* Half the water spilled from the test tube on her first try. *Again!* The second attempt went better, and the fifth held most of the intended sample.

She straightened, looked across the muddy banks. Rahul nodded in approval. Pride sprouted in her heart, tiny and bursting with life.

Two hours later, the veteran volunteers departed. Moena stood beside Rahul as he stored her samples in the trunk of his car. He, too, was stained with lake scum. Sweat matted his curls. Dirt caked his fingernails and cuticles. He handed her a bottle of water from a cooler.

Moena gulped half of it in seconds. It did little to ease the ache growing behind her eyes. Her sinuses throbbed.

Rahul frowned. 'Are you okay?' He gestured toward Moena's arms.

Patches of red blossomed everywhere that lake water had spattered on her.

'Allergies,' she said. 'I'll be fine.' *Liar, liar!*

'Then I'll thank you twice for helping. Not many people can handle this kind of work, and even fewer would sacrifice their health for it. Will I – will we, that is – see you next time?'

'Yes.'

Moena waited until she was in her car to blow her nose.

Syed glanced at her reflection in the rear-view mirror. 'Madam, why are you doing this to yourself?'

'Guilt, Syed! And love. Love for my people, the verdant ones and the fleshy ones and the ones you can only see under a microscope. Guilt that I've kept myself away for too long.'

————

The next week, Moena brought her own vials – empty and sterile – tucked in her jeans pockets. She wore a light cotton kameez with long sleeves. Scabbed patches decorated her skin, the after-effects of the previous session. While she worked, she collected her own samples of water and soil. Rahul might have been the catalyst for this madness, but the biota were the reactant that kept it fed.

She watched Rahul as he worked the nutrient tanks and pumps. His dark brow wrinkled in concentration, his jaw slack and lips parted, just enough for a peek of pink tongue. Green slime spattered his boots and the lower half of his jeans. *Brave, lovely man.*

He glanced up from his handheld – caught her staring. Moena's cheeks warmed as he smiled, tiny and knowing. *Concentrate!* The memory of his expression trickled down through her belly, lower, heating her, an exothermic reactor of her very own.

Once again, she and Rahul finished their work last. Syed had not yet returned from his tea break. She was about to message him to when Rahul spoke seven magic words: 'Would you like to get some coffee?'

Moena's inner fifteen-year-old jumped for joy, did

cartwheels, crowed to the world. A fit of coughing prevented her adult self from answering.

Gasping for breath, she said, 'Yes.'

She left the coffee untouched again. If Rahul noticed, he didn't comment, but he did ask her out to dinner. *Dinner – hurrah!* And yet not. *Idiot!* He would notice if she left an entire meal uneaten. The food would be crawling with microflora, with all the variety of Bangalore's citizens. Her stomach roiled at the thought. But she would do it – for Rahul, for the chance to fertilize the seeds of their relationship – anything for that.

———

'How was the date?' Ananya asked, smirking.

'Great! I spent the rest of the night on the toilet,' Moena said. 'But it was worth every minute. Rahul's so passionate about this work. Imagine what he's like in bed!'

The smile vanished from her friend's face. 'Don't joke! You can't keep risking your health for this. You should tell him the truth.'

'But he wants to see me again.'

'Stop stringing him along!'

'I can't. Besides, he's wrapped me in his own string package.'

'Oh, Mo, you've really fallen for him?'

'I'm still falling, drifting, like leaves in a Cambridge autumn. He can't ever know who I really am or he would grind me into the dirt.'

'You're not giving him enough credit. Either that, or he's an ass who doesn't deserve you.'

'You should see the cultures I'm getting from the lake.'

'What? Don't change the subject!'

'I think I've figured out a way to improve the breakdown of the polycarbonates. We need to change the nitrogen levels in the nutrient mix. Oh, and I spliced some enzyme sequences from *Geotrichum candidum* into the *flavobacterium* that's worked best so far.'

'Really? You were able to splice in fungal genes and the bacteria survived? Show me the data.'

They spent the rest of the conversation arguing over organic chemistry and whether a different strain or a second strain would make for a better solution. Moena went to bed dreaming of curing Bangalore's water ailments. What better token of love could she offer to Rahul?

―――

The baby bromeliads drooped. Their once dark green leaves faded, their tips browned. The house soil smelled like rotting cabbage in its shadier pockets. Two of the eBees kept crashing into the SmartWindows like drunks with frenetic wings.

Moena extracted samples from the surface and subsoil, ran them through the DNA sequencer. The lake bacteria had infiltrated her cultivated sanctum. They were winning.

She coughed over her shoulder and turned back to the scope. Her nose hadn't stopped dripping for weeks. At night, her joints ached. The coffin's masseuse software did little to relieve the pain.

But. But! Last night, five weeks after their first date and many a rendezvous since, she and Rahul had kissed. Wet bacteria-saliva-swapping glory! Her last boyfriend at Cambridge was a decade past. She'd forgotten how exquisite the dance of lips and tongue could be.

Rahul had whispered of his germinating passion: *There's no one in the world like you. The way you move, the way you talk – you're exquisite. You're my glorious once-blooming orchid.*

Those words! That metaphor!

The skin on the inside of her thighs burned, chafed from her numerous sessions with virtual-coffin-Rahul. Ten times ten times ten… The order of magnitude didn't matter. Ersatz satisfaction would never be enough. She needed the real thing.

Moena danced her gloved fingertips against the sterile tile countertop. Petri dishes and bottles of reagents crowded the glass-fronted refrigerator to her left. A jumble of live cultures and test tube racks littered the surface on her right, cosying up to the CRISPR-based gene editor.

She needed a solution to remediate the lake into health but also to heal her own biome. Every foray into the outside world – every handhold and kiss with Rahul – allowed new single-celled adversaries into the house.

To cut off contact with him? The idea was a nasty fly tiptoeing through the hairs of *Dionaea muscipula*. Snap, trap, digest! Banish it to nonexistence.

She exited her laboratory and padded to the southern side of the house. The sun-warmed grit under her bare feet helped her think. Never mind the arthritic curl bending her toes. *Fix the house, fix yourself.* She swabbed the leaves of a dwarf orange tree that was mottled with yellow and black spots.

'Wrong. Wrong. Wrong,' hummed the eBees.

Years to achieve balance. Weeks to fall apart. So unfair! Moena's inner five-year-old stomped and stormed and kicked up an unholy tantrum. Tears trickled. She wiped them away, catching some on the swab, contaminating it. *Idiot!*

She stumbled to her towering *Dieffenbachia* grove and curled up under the shade of their broad, variegated leaves. Her cheek sunk into the cool, soft loam. She extended her tongue – *wait!* How much beneficial microflora did the soil still have? Was it friend or foe?

To lick or not to lick? That is the question! Whether 'tis nobler in the mind to suffer the filth and rot of exterior living, or to take antibiotics – but that had too many syllables – against a sea of... *Damn.* She lost the analogy.

Moena giggled.

She beat her head against the ground. Madness. Her old friend had arrived for a visit. Let's catch up over chai. Plain or masala?

———

Ananya had left three messages, one for each call that Moena had ignored.

Soon. Soon she would return them. *Close!* She was so close to the answer. Her scalp itched. When had she last bathed? Not important. *Focus! There!* That snippet would turn her engineered bacteria into oxygen-devouring microbeasts. Bye-

bye, plastics! Nitrates as a by-product? Pretty please with citric acid on top, but only a dollop. Too much would be toxic.

Moena dumped the design into the artificial-life simulator. Crunch away! Tell me some good news! Please, please, let this combination be the magical one, the stable one.

The phone sang to her, that old Carnatic song about love birds. She'd assigned the tune to Rahul's caller ID. She had to answer.

'Meena, hi. Where are you? We're at the lake.'

'Oh.' She checked the calendar. Oh! *Focus! Be Meena again.* 'Sorry. I lost track of time.'

His image frowned on the tiny screen. Moena wanted to plant kisses in the adorable furrow between his brows.

'Are you okay? You don't look well.'

Damn. She hadn't meant to leave the camera on. *Distract him!*

'Hey, you're my boyfriend. You shouldn't say such things!'

Rahul's lips curved, frond-like. 'Am I your boyfriend now?'

Moena nodded, licked her lips. Promises, promises. 'I'll come soon. Will you be there in another hour?'

'The others won't, but I'll wait for you. I miss you.'

She returned to the simulation. *Go faster!* Numbers scrolled. Protein triplets sprinkled the results with alphabetic seeds. The probability of success ticked into the nineties. Good enough! Nothing yet had transcended the sixties. She kissed the screen, then transferred the design into the splicer.

Ten minutes later, Moena decanted half of her custom bacterial solution into a sterile test tube. *The solution is the solution!* She snickered. She pocketed that tube and took the remainder to the water feeder tank for the house. *Be fruitful and multiply, my little beasties!* You will save the soil, the house, *me*.

————

The sun's glare reflected from the lake, stabbing through Moena's eyes and into her frontal cortex like an illuminated knife. *Light sensitivity!* Another symptom of her degrading health.

Never mind! Salvation lay in her pocket. She slipped a finger in, caressed the glass tube. Her mind wandered to another cylindrical object, one that wasn't so cold and brittle.

Rahul stood by the pump. Sweat beaded on his forehead, dewdrops on buttery leather. He motioned her over. He'd already taught her how to work the injection well and nutrient tank. All she had to do today was pour in her vial when he wasn't looking.

The single-celled lovelies would digest the iron and polycarbonates in the water, then make their way into the locals. The guts of Bangalore – human and animal – would shit out more of Moena's microbabies. They would infect the sewage runoff and restore the water to liveable purity.

She stumbled over the slight rise of the concrete pad. Fire blazed up from her rheumatic toes to her swollen knees. Rahul caught her before she fell. She gasped as his hands crushed the weeping sores under her sleeves. *Bite your tongue! Don't scream!*

'What's the matter?'

Spin a lie, quick! Before he can think.

'Sprained my ankle, that's all.'

She plucked her arm from his grasp, staggered to the nutrient tank, pried off the lid.

'What are you doing?'

No more time for subterfuge. No time to talk. Her body would give out soon.

The stench from the fomenting cultures flowed into Moena's nostrils, triggered the nausea-inducing portion of her brain. Her stomach contracted. *No time!*

She yanked the vial from her pocket. *Splash!* In went her microbes.

Uncontrolled experiment! Her advisor's voice rang in her head. *Unpublished! Unverified! Dangerous!*

Sorry, Professor.

Concrete bashed Moena's knees as she knelt and vomited. War raged in her gut. Which side would prevail? Red and black streaked the mess that splattered across the dull grey cement.

'Meena!'

Rahul's head blocked the sun. Golden light haloed his black curls.

'Surya,' she whispered. Sun God. Beautiful.

She heaved again. Tremors coursed through her major muscle groups. She was a tree in a storm, her core rotted through by maggots. She toppled.

Rahul/Surya scooped her up, carried her to the car. Syed's voice and his swirled with frantic concern. Her own protests joined in admixture, dilute and ineffective.

Stop! You can't bring him home!
Blackness overtook Moena's vision.

————

Blurs of light. Sticky eyelids. Puffy tongue. Somewhere, an incessant annoying *beep beep beep.*

Moena shifted her arm. Warning pain: *a needle.* She blinked. The world resolved, focused, magnified – like looking through a giant drop of water. A bag of clear fluid fed into a tube.

Intravenous drip. She inclined her head. She was in her bedroom, alone, and being fed by this device. *Contamination.* Who had been in her house? What miserable microbes crawled in with them? What were they feeding her?

Antibiotics. The label confirmed it. They were poisoning her, killing her microscopic friends, the colonies she'd worked so long to build.

Moena extracted the needle. She licked at the pearl of blood that formed, pressed on the hole with her thumb. *Beep. Beep.* There: her tablet bleated from her desk. The world spun and swayed as she walked and dropped into the chair.

Low battery. She silenced the alarm, sucked away another drop of blood, plugged the device in. An indicator light flashed in the upper corner: Rahul had left her a message. Video. She played it.

His face appeared on the screen. Drooping, but lovely. Kissable lips that moved with care.

'They wouldn't let me in. Syed called your physician. She took care of you, said you had to be isolated in your home or you wouldn't get well. Meena – sorry, Moena – I don't know what else to say. I always suspected that you were hiding something, but this? It's too much. I don't understand you. What do you want with someone like me? Sex? A lower class boy to toy with until you find someone in your own circles? Did you think I wouldn't mind because I'm a guy? Well, you were wrong. You broke my heart.'

Anger, disappointment, betrayal – the lines of his face grew harder, twisted, a tree grown without enough water.

'I changed my mind,' she whispered at the screen. 'I wanted everything about you, in the end.'

She brushed away a tear and traced his image with the wet finger, blurring his features, softening them. *You don't understand what I am.* She pressed 'record', to explain, to rip out the lies and plant the truth in his ears, but no sound emerged. How could words be enough?

The silence crushed Moena. Tears slipped, spattered, diluted the blood welling on the back of her hand. She stumbled from the bedroom into the glaring sunshine of the main house.

'Your fault. Your fault,' droned the eBees.

She headed for the *Dieffenbachia* grove. The test plants stood straight, verdant and white, not a patch of yellow or brown. Translucent pink worms writhed away from her curling toes. The earth under Moena's feet felt crumbly and cool, and the sweet scent of compost filled the air.

'At least I saved you,' she said. She caressed the waxy leaves with her fingertips. 'My darlings, you still love me, don't you? You'll help me.'

Moena lay down, wiped the bloody smear on the back of one hand into the dirt, wiped her cheeks with the other. She licked the dark streak of loam from her skin. The bitterness of blood mixed with rich manganese and the tang of humic acid. She pinched the soil between her fingertips. She needed to analyse it. If this grove was thriving, she could help the other parts of the house.

And Rahul? How to remediate a polluted relationship? His love had wrapped Moena with its brambles, dug into her flesh, held tight. Pulling them out would leave her riddled with holes.

Did he hurt this much, too? *My heart is broken*, he'd said. She didn't have the strength to think it through. First, she had to heal herself.

———

One week fell away, then another, then a third. The house became a safe haven rather than hostile territory. Leaves returned to verdurous states. The eBees whirled in sober coordination. Moena's thoughts became as clear as her SmartWindows.

'You need to make a peace offering, a gift,' Ananya said. 'But then what? Will he be willing to live on your terms? I'm sorry, Mo. I wish you could find that kind of happiness, but maybe Rahul isn't the right one.'

A gift – a token of love. What mattered most to Rahul? This city. Its water. Its land. Moena could give him the health of Bangalore, but only if she knew whether her experiment had worked.

This time she wore the isolation suit to the lake. She avoided the volunteer hours. The water stretched like grey glass, rippled by the occasional crow's feet. Her breath rasped through the filters. Strange, not to smell anything. Moena scooped samples from the water and the lake bed, carried them back to the car where Syed waited, his face wrinkled with concern.

The results were gorgeous. The polycarbonate levels had dropped well below the previous curve. She needed more data over time to measure the new rate, but this was enough for an initial publication. Her hands quivered like stamens in a breeze. She typed for ten hours, loaded the draft on to a data cube. Gene sequences and a vial of live cultures completed the package.

Moena sat in the citrus grove. She inhaled the aroma of orange blossoms and traced curlicues in the sandy soil. A tablet lay by her feet. It displayed the feed from the door camera. Syed picked up the padded envelope and disappeared.

Would Rahul answer? Would he understand? Would he forgive?

The draft paper described her life down to its deepest roots. The seeds of health – for her, for everyone – were sown throughout the dry, technical paragraphs. She sent a second copy to Ananya. Let Professor Das lend it credibility. Let their ideas infect the world. Let Rahul come back to her life.

Moena waited three days. Nothing. Not a call or message or note. He had pruned her away like a rotten branch. Poison. That's what her actions had brought to his life and her own. She deserved to be cut off.

Moena took a kitchen knife to the coffin. She drew it through the supple fabric lining, parting it like the skin of a ripe tomato. Wires, actuators, and pressure sensors burst forth in an overgrown tangle. *Begone, temptation!*

She drew the blade through it once more the next day and the day after. For each twenty-four hours that Rahul didn't answer, she slashed another reminder of what she was: moron, idiot, lunatic. *Never again!*

Rahul arrived on the day she made the fourteenth stroke. He looked nothing like a repairman. He wore a loose kurta and baggy cotton pants. His curls had grown, and they blew like errant wood shavings around his face. A nylon bag rested by his feet.

'Miss...Sivaram?' he said through the intercom. He flashed his crooked smile.

Moena buried a rising sob. 'I'm coming.'

She ran through sunlight and shade, leaves and fronds

caressing her bare arms, urging her forward. *Go! Faster!* She stopped at the inner threshold of the foyer.

'I'm so sorry, Rahul. About all of it. I didn't know how else –'

'It's okay. I read your paper. I understood enough, I think. I had H.E.G. do the lab analysis on your samples and the lake. My God, Moena, the water there is incredible! What a transformation! The work you've done – it could change everything.' He paused. 'Can I come in?'

Unshed tears suffused Moena's face, filled the cavities, pushed her into action. She opened the outer door as her answer. Rahul removed his shoes and walked in. She set the sterilizing wash to a simple soap solution.

'Close your eyes,' she said.

Water drenched Rahul like a personal cloudburst. Rivulets of brown ran into the drain, washing away dust and oil and the hostility of Bangalore. Wet cloth delineated the contours of his body.

Moena retrieved a towel from her bedroom. The mutilated coffin sat to one side, an eyesore.

Shame rooted her feet. Cover it up? *No.* No more secrets. She returned to Rahul as the wash ended.

'I'm sorry I was silent for so long,' he said. 'At first I was waiting for the lab results, and then I had to make some arrangements in case...'

'Of what?' she prompted.

'In case you'll have me to stay.'

'You mean...in here, with me?'

He nodded. Crystal clear droplets fell from his hair.

'I'm not normal, Rahul. I never will be. That's why I didn't tell you who I was. It wasn't about the money or your caste. How could I ask you to fall in love with the insanity of my house, my life? I can't offer a wedding or children or happy occasions with the whole family. All I have is money and isolation.'

'And the beauty of your intellect. Your generous spirit. Your passion for the earth.' Rahul's eyes glistened. 'Moena, you are the strangest, most wonderful human being I've ever known. How could I not be hopelessly in love with you? I don't care about weddings and children. You have the power to change the world, and I want to be part of that, to be part of your life.'

'You'll have to stay inside for a long time.'

'I know.'

'It could be months or even years until I can stabilize the biome for both of us.'

'I can accept that.'

'And your family?'

He laughed, crooked teeth flashing. 'They've given up on me. Over thirty, unmarried, and volunteering in cesspools – they think I'm crazy.'

The Carnatic love birds crooned.

'Then let's be lunatics together,' she said.

She opened the inner door. It closed behind Rahul with a slight sucking noise, not unlike a kiss. *Hush! Be patient!* She took him by the hand and led him to the elephant ear tree. Their bare feet left two sets of prints in the rich, dark soil.

Rahul gazed up into the canopy. Sunshine and wonderment dappled his face.

'Meet your father,' Moena whispered to the baby bromeliads.

She crouched and ran a finger through the soil. He knelt beside her.

'Open your mouth,' she said.

Rahul's brow quirked in puzzlement. His lips parted. Moena's finger hovered, then darted between like a hummingbird's beak, depositing its microbial pollen on his waiting tongue. His eyes opened wide and white as forbidden jasmine.

'Your first inoculation,' she whispered.

His mouth surrounded her finger, sucking gently. His teeth tickled her skin.

The eBees hummed, 'Kiss him! Kiss him!'

The leaves rustled in agreement. *Now!*

Moena freed her hand and twined her arms around Rahul's neck. She pressed her trunk into his, then her lips. The damp heat of his body soaked into hers. His flavours purled across her tongue. Lingering grit. Chilli powder. Kernels of salt. Their microbiota swirled, integrated, danced into each other, merged into one biomass. *What's yours is mine. What's mine is yours.*

'Welcome home,' Moena said.

AN UNEXPECTED BOON

Kalyani had to stop and touch the Jambu trees lining the road, each exactly twice, or else her insides would itch. She counted as she walked.

'Twelve. Fourteen. Sixteen,' she murmured, tapping the bark lightly with the pad of her index finger.

'Hurry up,' Aruni said.

Her brother was three years older and one hundred steps ahead. Kalyani was twelve. She could have kept up with him if it weren't for the trees.

They arrived at school on time. Kalyani kept track of the sun's position so she could pace herself. When they passed into the stone enclosure, she flipped her long, black braid to the front and stroked it with her left hand. One stroke for each step; one to sit cross-legged on the packed dirt; one for each of the students around her. The boys had their hair coiled in top-knots. She was glad to be a girl with hair hanging in reach.

The guru asked a boy to recite the Rig Veda from the fourth mandala and fourth hymn. Four by four was sixteen, one of Kalyani's favourite numbers. She knew the words by heart: 'Make your vigour like a wide spreading net. Go like a mighty king with your host following in the rapid passage of your march. You are the archer. Transfix the fiends with your most burning shafts.'

She had memorized all the Vedas. The guru stopped asking her for recitations years ago, around the same time the other children refused to play with her.

After their instruction was finished for the day, she waited by the road for her brother. Aruni stood near Urmila, his intended bride. He spoke to her at least four times a day at school. Sometimes eight. Never ten, not since the time Kalyani screamed at him for it. Ten was unlucky.

'Kalyani, want to come with me to the mango grove?'

One of the older boys stood in front of her and smiled with lots of teeth. Smiles were good. Aruni was always telling her to smile more often. But she wasn't fond of mangoes.

'Are there birds?' she asked. Birds – and animals in general – were easier to understand than people. They didn't make her insides itch with their gazes.

'Birds?' He paused, smiled wider. 'Sure, why not.'

'Okay.'

She followed him across the road and down a short path. A few other students were scattered about, always in felicitous groups of two. Several pairs had already been promised in marriage. She peered up at the leafy branches.

The boy's arm wrapped around her waist from behind.

Kalyani shrieked and pushed him away so hard that he stumbled and fell. Her skin itched with the memory of his arm, and she couldn't stop her shrill cries as she scratched desperately.

Aruni came running, yelling at the boy, asking him what he'd done.

'She followed me here,' the boy retorted. 'Everyone knows what the mango grove means! It's not my fault your sister is crazy!'

'She doesn't like to be touched,' Aruni said. 'Everybody knows that, too!'

Kalyani clapped four times and ran, the raised voices fading as she gained distance. The itch penetrated inward from her skin as she fled past the Jambu trees. The need to get home – familiar, safe – overwhelmed all other considerations. Her feet slapped on the dirt road – *thwap, thock* – even, odd. Her ankle bells chimed. *Trink. Trank.* She arrived at their house out of breath, remembered to step across the threshold with her right foot.

Chithra, the black cat, sauntered over and rubbed against her legs. Kalyani squatted and stroked her. The plush fur whispered, cool and silken, against her burning palm.

'One, two, three, four,' she whispered.

She forgot to count in pairs. The damage was done. Her insides crawled with itches she could not reach, but she kept petting, kept counting, hoping for relief. She was at 'two-hundred forty-three' when Aruni arrived. It was not an auspicious number.

'What were you thinking, going off with him by yourself?'

'He said he would show me birds. He smiled at me. You said smiles are good!'

'Not all smiles are the same, Kala. How are you going to find a husband if you can't even figure that much out?'

'Two-hundred fifty-seven,' Kalyani murmured.

Her brother sighed. Sighs were never good.

Kalyani settled on the dirt, curling her body around Chithra's. She inhaled the animal's calming musk. People were too complicated, their gazes inscrutable, their touch demanding and fiery. Life would be easier if she could marry an animal.

———

Aruni fumed on the way to the cooking area in the back. Someone had to prepare their afternoon meal, and Kalyani was useless when it came to housework, especially in her current state. Why did his sister have to be so strange? The adults in their village tolerated her fits, but their schoolmates had less patience.

He would be happier once their parents came home. Father's latest play was being performed across the river, in the grand city of Prayag, and for the first time Mother had gone with him, leaving Aruni in charge of their household. He was old enough, and he thought he would enjoy the freedom. He'd forgotten to account for his sister.

After he cooked the rice and lentil stew, he worked on his mural. The afternoon sun cast a pleasing, mellow light over the half-finished landscape. He frowned at the nearly empty pot of red dye. It was the most expensive colour, and Father wouldn't be selling any of their cattle for months. How could he perfectly capture the setting sun without red?

His thoughts were interrupted by a man calling from the front of the house. A sage, clad in loin-cloth and a bead necklace, stood in the yard. White hair hung to his hips, and his beard reached the middle of his wrinkled, sun-browned chest.

They were used to receiving travellers – their house being the closest to the bridge from Prayag – but this was the first time with Mother away.

'Be welcome, sir,' Aruni said. He ushered the man onto their stone veranda and went to find Kalyani.

His sister stood by a tree, running her fingers along the back of a chipmunk.

'Kala, there's a sage in front. Mother's gone, so you'll have to serve him.'

His sister followed him to the well where he washed a banana leaf and handed it to her along with a clay cup filled with water.

'I know what to do,' she said. 'I've watched Mother.'

Aruni bit at his cuticles and watched from the back of the house. Light filtered through their thatched roof and made criss-cross patterns on the beaten dirt floor. A fly droned past his ear. He groaned as his sister served the guest half the food he had cooked, but the traveller's needs took priority.

Sometimes a wandering ascetic was just that, but Aruni knew the stories. The more devoted sages had power given by the gods. What if Kalyani, with her strange ways, caused offence to someone like that? He wished that Mother were here to handle it.

The sage finished eating in silence. His sister sat and stared at nothing in her peculiar way. After Kalyani had cleared the meal and brought a wash pot, she knelt and prostrated to the sage. To Aruni's relief, the old man smiled and said something to his sister. The words were too soft for him to hear.

Then, miraculously, Kalyani replied. The man spoke again, and his sister held out her hand. The sage put something into it. Aruni danced with curiosity, but he dared not interrupt whatever was going on.

The sage looked through the house, straight at Aruni, who stopped fidgeting, then nodded in thanks and departed. After the traveller had passed out of their gate and turned down the road – toward their village and onward to the city, most likely – Aruni breathed a sigh of relief.

Kalyani hadn't moved.

He ran to her. 'What did he say? Show me what he gave you!'

She opened her hand. An iridescent black beetle nestled in her palm. Its wings shimmered with fern-like emerald and morning glory purple. The tail was a lighter colour, almost clear.

'What is that for?'

'The sage offered me a boon.'

'A boon! Why?'

'He said that I was quiet and he liked not being chattered at.'

'You could have asked for anything, Kala! You wanted an insect?'

'I asked for a friend. This is a magic lightning beetle. His name is Mithraba. The sage said so. He said I can use Mithraba as a token of entry.'

'To where?'

'His ashram.'

Aruni snorted. A useless offer – their parents needed help at home. He couldn't study art with the masters in Prayag, and Kalyani would never be sent to live in an ashram. He took the insect from his sister's hand to examine it more closely.

Kalyani shrieked.

'Don't touch him,' she cried. She was scratching at her palm, and her ribcage swelled in readiness for a fit.

'Sorry! Here, open your hand!' He dropped the beetle into her outstretched palm, carefully avoiding contact.

She clutched the creature against her heart and ran into the thicket across the lane. Aruni shook his head. Why would the sage give her a beetle? Better that he'd cured her of this madness.

———

Kalyani kept Mithraba close over the next few days and nights, watching the lightning beetle's glow. She decoded his yes and no patterns on the first night: Two light flashes meant yes; one was no.

At her request, Aruni had made exaggerated faces at her – happy, sad, angry – until she memorized those patterns. Mithraba flashed other patterns and sometimes beat his wings for certain counts, too. She wasn't sure yet what they meant, but she kept a chart in her head of everything that she'd seen. She loved riddles.

Today was market day, which Kalyani normally skipped because of the crowds. Her skin would itch for hours afterwards, and she would sit near their well, scratching and screaming and dousing herself with water. With their parents being gone, though, she had to help her brother.

'Twenty-four. Twenty-six,' she murmured.

The Jambu trees dwindled to nothing at the outskirts of the village. If she could be a tree, she would rather be a fragrant Parijatha with its star-white flowers that only opened at night.

Night was better than day. Less light and sound meant less itching in her thoughts.

They arrived at the chaos of men, women, animals, and baskets. Kalyani's skin tingled. She kept her braid in back and stroked Mithraba instead. She had tucked the beetle into the folds of her cotton sari, right near her breastbone. He liked feeling her heart beat. He flashed his tail four times to tell her so.

Their first stop was the coconut-oil maker. The woman smiled at Kalyani with red-stained teeth. The colour was from the chewing of betel leaves, but if all smiles weren't the same, what did this one mean?

Mithraba flapped his wings twice: friendliness.

Kalyani hazarded a quiet, 'Namaste.'

The oil vendor kept smiling, but Aruni scrunched his brow. Was he angry or deep in thought?

Mithraba did five flashes and four flaps. It wasn't a code she knew.

'I'm surprised you talked to her,' Aruni said when they walked on. He handed her the clay jar full of oil.

She made a note in her mental chart: five flashes plus four flaps equals surprise.

'Six, seven, eight, nine.' Kalyani counted the steps to the next stall. Unsettled by the odd number, she took a small step back. Nine minus one was eight. Much better.

They were at the venison dealer. He smiled, too. Mithraba flapped three times. Kalyani didn't eat meat because it made her insides itch, but Aruni and her parents did. They never let it touch her banana leaves.

She was glad when they moved on. Fruits and vegetables were less itchy.

Voices clashed as vendors called out their wares. *Cluck-clack*, cried the chickens. A horse whinnied, and a goat bleated.

Kalyani's ears itched inside and out. She was carrying too much to scratch them or to stroke Mithraba so she rubbed them against her shoulders.

Their pace slowed. They stopped, but not at a vendor. She lifted her gaze to discover that Aruni was speaking with Urmila.

'My parents want to speak to yours when they return,' Urmila said. 'I think they want to set a wedding date.'

Aruni smiled. 'At last! Mother and Father are due back in two days. I'll tell them as soon as I see them.'

'Meanwhile Father is trying to convince my younger brother to become a well-builder, but he wants to be a cow-herder like you.'

'Really? Cattle are so tedious. If I could do anything, I would be a painter.'

Urmila scrunched up her face, and Kalyani glanced down at Mithraba. He gave her an unfamiliar pattern.

'I'm glad you raise cattle,' Urmila said. 'I'd rather stay here and be close to my family than go live in the capital. Besides, you can still paint here.'

Aruni smiled. Happy, Mithraba indicated, but also sad. Kalyani checked her mental chart to confirm that she hadn't made a mistake.

She hadn't.

'I could study painting with the masters in Prayag if my parents had another son,' Aruni said. 'Oh, you should come to the house soon. I'll show you the new scene I've added.'

'I will.'

And then Urmila was looking right at Kalyani who immediately dropped her gaze. Eyes were like wells; they made her dizzy if she stared into their depths for too long. Urmila's were particularly challenging, with their dark kajal outlines and shiny collyrium on the lids.

'How is that cat you keep, Kalyani? Has she had kittens yet?'

'No, it's the wrong season for kittens.'

Urmila blinked.

Mithraba was still and dark.

Kalyani itched everywhere. Urmila's stare made it hard for her to breathe.

'I have to go home,' Kalyani gasped.

As she hurried away, Aruni apologized to Urmila. He did that a lot. She didn't understand why. She glanced down, but Mithraba was no help.

———

Each day without Mother and Father had tested Aruni's patience: with his sister, with housework, and with mud from the rains. He had to endure one more day until their scheduled return.

The trip to the market had gone surprisingly well. Kalyani claimed her magic beetle could help her understand people better. After yesterday's behaviour at the market, he was almost willing to believe her. His sister's abruptness had startled Urmila at the end, but his betrothed was forgiving. She had to be if she was going to live with them as his wife, at least until Kalyani was married and gone.

Aruni's shoulders ached and his palms chafed as he drew water from their well. The hempen rope was miserably wet, and mud coated every surface, making his feet slip on the stone steps to the house. He almost dropped the clay pot full of water. The rain was unusual for this time of year, and he looked forward to a bath in the cistern, which had been dry for weeks.

He heard his sister speaking. Had Mother and Father returned early? He strode through the house, heedless of the muddy footprints in his wake. Another wandering wise man – a much younger one this time, with black hair and smooth skin – stood on the veranda with Kalyani. She proffered a cup of water while staring intently at the beetle in her sari.

'Stay still! Don't be afraid,' the man said, reaching toward Kalyani.

He plucked the beetle and crushed it between his fingers. Kalyani screamed.

The cup fell from her hand, its coconut shell clacking as it rolled across the stone floor.

Aruni froze.

Kalyani collapsed on the muddy stone veranda and howled like the world had ended. Perhaps it had. The sage towered over her and frowned. Annoyance built on his face, and Aruni forced himself to move.

'I apologize for my sister, sir,' he said, raising his voice over hers.

'Why is she shrieking like a demoness?'

'That beetle was a pet, sir.'

The sage's brow furrowed deeper. 'I thought she was frightened of it. It was a well-intentioned mistake, but it's only an insect. She can get another one.'

Kalyani clawed at her stomach. Her piercing wails continued.

'Will she stop?'

'I don't think so, sir, not very soon.' Aruni felt near to tears. Kalyani's distressing noise was bad enough, but now the traveller looked to be angry with them. 'Might I serve you?'

'You insult me!' he thundered. 'I would not be sullied that way, and I can hardly eat with this racket.'

Aruni fell to knees, touched the sage's feet. 'I meant no disrespect. Please –'

But the sage stepped away. He looked down at Kalyani. 'Will you not behave, girl? Do you know what I think of such inhospitable behaviour?'

Aruni trembled at the rage on the other man's face. *Please, merciful gods, let my sister recover!* The unearthly shrieks continued.

'Then I curse this house. As you have rejected me from your home, so shall yours turn you out!'

He flung the beetle's misshapen mass at Kalyani and stalked out into the rain. The insect landed on Kalyani's outstretched palm. Her eyes snapped open, and she took a deep breath.

'Don't cry,' Aruni said quickly. 'I'll burn it for you.'

The ritual honour and purification of fire was for family, but it was the only act of solace he could think of.

'No,' Kalyani said. 'I won't be parted from Mithraba.'

She popped the dead insect into her mouth and swallowed. 'He's mine,' she said as she stood and walked to the front gate. 'Forever.'

'Where are you going? Didn't you hear what he said? He cursed us! You can't just walk away! Because of you and that damned bug of yours, we're doomed to be homeless. Kalyani, come back!'

She crossed the lane and disappeared into a haze of rain and trees. Aruni smashed a fist against the stone floor and sat back. Rainwater soaked through his threadbare dhoti in seconds. He pulled up his knees and rested his head and arms on them.

I'm a man now. I can take care of everything, he had promised his parents. *Don't worry. We'll be fine.*

But they weren't fine. He was only a boy after all.

Aruni sat on the porch until he was stiff and cold. A chill wind blew in as the sun set. He should have cooked some food, but he couldn't stop thinking about the traveller's words. What would it mean for them?

The day's light faded behind dark grey clouds, and still Kalyani had not returned. Why did he have to be burdened with such a sister? His parents must have done something wrong to deserve a child such as her. Or perhaps it was his fault from a past life.

Mud coated his feet as Aruni crossed the lane. He had to bring Kalyani home before night fell. Familiar trails became strange in the half-light of dusk. Raindrops pattered on the broad canopies above him. Deep shadows filled every gap, but the smells of wet earth and greenery were rich and calming.

He tried Kalyani's usual haunts first: the grassy stream bank where she liked to wash her feet; the glade of white-barked trees where she fed the chipmunks. His sister wasn't anywhere he looked. Heavy drops tapped his head constantly, and mud sucked at his tired feet. *Idiot girl.* Had she managed to get lost? How would he find her in the dark? He glanced up at the gloom. If he didn't find her soon, he wouldn't be able to make his way home.

He continued on as long as he dared without seeing or hearing anything but ferns, trees, and water. With a sinking heart, he turned toward home. How would he explain this failure, on top of the others, to his parents? Every step felt like stone weights were tied to his legs.

I tried my best. It's not my fault if my sister is crazy and gets herself lost in the jungle at night. Serves her right if she gets eaten by tiger! All this over a stupid beetle. Oh Brihaspati, please give my sister some sense, and holy Varuna, please stop sending us travellers until Mother comes home.

Aruni emerged from the forest. A glow lit the side of the house, beyond his line of sight. Had their parents come home at last? He quickened his steps across the lane. Was it a fire? But no wood would catch on such a wet night.

He rounded the corner and stumbled to a stop. Kalyani lay on the ground, covered in mud, a serene expression on her face. A spotted leopard stretched out beside her. Its eyes were half-closed as his sister stroked it from head to tail.

Kalyani glowed.

Her whole body emitted a soft yellow light. Wherever cracks of skin showed through the mud, she blazed. She looked as if the sun itself burned within her; like goddess Usha at dawn.

Aruni fell to the ground and prostrated himself.

'What are you doing?' Kalyani asked, sitting up.

'Paying my respects,' he choked out.

'It's all Mithraba's magic. I'm not holy.'

Aruni raised his upper body cautiously. 'And the leopard?'

Kalyani's hand rested casually on the animal's back.

'Mithraba makes it easier for me to understand all living things.' She glanced at Aruni, then down to her chest as if the beetle still rested by her heart. 'He says you're afraid. I'll ask my friend to go.'

She leaned and whispered into the leopard's ear, which twitched once before the great cat – nearly twice as large as Kalyani – stood, stretched, and loped away.

Aruni willed his heart to slow down. 'What now?'

'I'm hungry,' Kalyani said.

'I...haven't cooked anything. I was looking for you.'

'I'm sorry,' Kalyani said. It was the first apology he had heard from her. 'I'll make something.'

He was going to protest that it was too dark to cook and then realized the foolishness of his words. Light stood before him. He shook his head in wonderment. The Vedas told far stranger tales, but Aruni never expected to be living in one.

'I'll cook.' He smiled. 'But you have to light the way.'

———

Scrape. Scrape. Scrape.

Kalyani's nails left red streaks on her skin as they scrubbed away last night's mud. She was careful to use her four fingers, not the odd-numbered thumb.

Aruni stood next to her in the cistern, also washing. Her brother stretched his long brown limbs and smiled. Light pulsed faintly through the wet cotton folds across her chest: four times; his smile was happy.

Splash-splosh went the water as he waded out. Urmila's voice called out his name.

'We're in the back,' Aruni yelled. 'Come around!'

Her brother's future wife arrived breathless. Her skin shone with sweat. 'The bridge washed out! The river water swelled and came rushing. My father told us. He was about to cross over to Prayag. He thinks the dam upstream must have broken.'

Too bad, Kalyani thought. She liked the bridge and its twelve stone pillars. It connected their village to the capital city where their parents had gone. Kalyani scrubbed the last of the mud from between her toes.

'How is he?' Aruni was saying. 'Anyone hurt?'

Kalyani climbed out of the cistern and walked toward the house to put on a dry sari.

'A few people.' Urmila lowered her voice. 'Three of them died. They blame *her*.'

Kalyani stopped. Aruni and Urmila were looking at her, and their gazes made hot spots on her skin.

'What does the bridge have to do with Kala?'

'A sage came through the village yesterday. He was so angry, Aruni. He told people that your sister is cursed.'

Kalyani's insides began to itch, and a scream built as the sensation became unbearable. She dropped to her hands and knees and screamed, but no sound emerged. Light spilled from her open mouth. It pooled on the packed dirt and then vanished like water being sucked into the ground.

'What is she doing? Is it true, then, what he said?'

Kalyani clutched and clawed at the burning in her stomach. Tears of pain dribbled off her chin and fell as glowing drops.

'I – I'm not sure. She's become something strange. Full of light. That can't be bad, right? There was another sage, before the one from last night, and he gave her a lightning beetle as a boon.'

Kalyani's palms flashed thrice. She felt five wing-beats against her breastbone from the inside. Aruni and Urmila were sad and frightened. Or maybe she was. The itching abated.

'Never mind, Aruni! It doesn't matter who did what. Look at her! If the villagers see that, I don't know what they would do. Please, you have to take her and leave before they get here.'

First Mithraba's death, and now this. She couldn't swallow everyone she loved.

Wing-beats drummed a complicated pattern inside her. She recalled what the old sage had said when he'd handed Mithraba over. Would he honour his token if it was a ghost within her?

———

Aruni's heart nearly stopped at Urmila's plea. 'Take my sister and go? Aren't you coming? You're my bride!'

'I can't.' Tears trailed black kajol down her cheeks. 'We're not married yet.'

'We've promised ourselves to each other. We can get married somewhere else, in Prayag maybe. We'll find my parents there. They'll help.'

'You're asking me to leave my family with no assurances? I can't do that! My first duty is to them!'

Aruni balled his hands into fists. Mother and Father were gone. He was being turned out of his home. Kalyani had become something unearthly. Urmila was all he had left, and she was abandoning him, too.

'Fine, we'll go,' he said. 'Run off and tell the ones who are coming for us.'

'Don't be like that! I came to help you.'

'Thank you,' he said. He folded his hands and bowed formally. 'I'll handle it from here.'

He ignored the stab of guilt at Urmila's devastated expression before she turned away. He couldn't afford softer feelings now. Kalyani alternately vomited light and stared at her hands. As usual, she was no help. He stepped around her and gathered a spare dhoti, his paint pots, and brushes. What else should he take? He'd never been beyond the village limits. How was he supposed to know what to do?

A small, cool hand rested on his bare shoulder. Startled, he turned and saw his sister standing behind him. Light leaked faintly from her eyes, nose, ears, lips.

'Follow me.'

Kalyani walked away, her anklets tinkling. He stared at her back for two astonished breaths, then grabbed the cloth bundle and ran after her. Why not? If she was touched by the gods, perhaps she had an idea of what to do.

They headed toward the river. Sunbeams reached the treetops, outlining the leaves in gold. The forest birds cried out in a raucous chorus. Faint human voices carried through them. Aruni looked back, but the villagers were out of sight.

'We should move off the road, Kala.'

She nodded and took them on an overgrown forest path. Ferns brushed their legs. Vines drooped with aromatic white and yellow flowers from above. A faint, warm mist formed as the day warmed, and Aruni began to sweat.

Then he smelled smoke.

'Kalyani, stop!'

He climbed up a tree. Smoke rose in writhing columns from the thatched roof of their home.

'The house is burning,' he said.

'And the fields?'

'They will catch fire soon.'

Kalyani dashed through the undergrowth.

'Wait for me!'

Aruni scrambled down the trunk. He caught up to his sister at the wooden fence that enclosed their pastures.

'What's the matter with you? When you first got that beetle, I thought it was going to make you normal, but you're crazier than ever!'

'Mithraba is still with me, and I will always be myself.' Her eyes glowed. 'We have to save the cattle. Help me!'

The half-rotted planks came loose with a few hard tugs. Kalyani ran through the gap. His sister's whole body glowed by the time they reached the herd. She whispered into a few rounded ears, then headed back the way they came. He followed her, as did the cattle, their musky bodies pressing into him. His sister led the way through the broken fence.

Kalyani motioned him into the cover of the forest. The animals lowed and squeezed through the gap, a few at a time, until more sections splintered from their bulk. Their father's wealth ambled away in front of their eyes, and Aruni could do nothing to stop it. He should have remembered the cattle. He should have come up with a better plan to save them, hidden them somewhere they could be found. He hadn't meant to be such a disappointment.

The line of flame was visible now, a flickering orange-red that answered the steady glow beside him.

'They'll be safe,' Kalyani said. 'We should go.'

They reached the river south of the collapsed bridge. A bend in its course hid them from view and blocked the great city of Prayag from their sight. Aruni examined his body and pulled off several small leeches. His sister was untouched.

The red clay of the riverbank stretched ahead for several strides before it disappeared into the placid green water. Here and there, a nubby grey-green snout poked above the surface.

'We'll cross here and then walk to Prayag,' Kalyani said.

'Have you lost your mind? Even if we could swim the entire width, those gharials would eat us alive.'

'No, they won't.'

Kalyani tied her sari between her legs and waded into the water, her glow visible in spite of the blazing sunlight. The brilliant combination made him squint.

His sister held out her hands and waited until two snouts nosed against them. She reached past the rounded tips to stroke the long, straight sections of the gharials' muzzles. Then she walked slowly backwards, leading them out of the water.

Aruni's throat constricted as the two enormous reptiles emerged. Each was at least three times his height in length. The narrow snouts with bulbous caps made them easily distinguishable from their cousins.

'They'll carry us across.'

'You...want to ride...on these?' he whispered.

Kalyani frowned. 'You're afraid.'

'Look at the size of them! They could break our legs with one bite.'

His sister cocked her head. 'They're my friends now. They wouldn't do that.'

Aruni rubbed his temples. Should he listen to her? His sister was a child. She might have inhuman powers, but that didn't make her wise. He closed his eyes against her dazzling form so he could think.

'It's too dangerous,' he said. 'We're better off going further downriver where no one knows us and where we might find another bridge.'

'The sage said Mithraba is a token to enter his ashram. We'll be safe there. I can study. You can paint. But we have to collect Mother and Father first. We have to go through Prayag. This crossing will take us almost as close to the city as our bridge.'

Her words were surprisingly sensible. Kalyani would make a good scholar, with her near-perfect memory and skill in mathematics. The ashram might welcome his Father's play-writing skills. Mother could help tend their garden.

And he would have the freedom to paint.

If only Urmila had come with them, it would have been a perfect situation.

Smoke blew from the forest's edge and made him cough. The crackle of flames was close enough to be audible. What choice did they really have?

'Holy Varuna,' Aruni prayed, 'please give us safe passage across the river, through Prayag, and to the sage's ashram.' He turned to Kalyani and nodded. 'I'm ready.'

With a mixture of terror and awe, he climbed astride the gharial that was closer to him. Its back was hard and scaly but also warm and solid. As they swam into the river, he twisted around to watch the shore recede. They were leaving the only home they'd known.

'Mithraba says you're sad. Is it because of Urmila?'

Aruni breathed into the sudden tightness of his chest.

'I liked her, Kala. I thought we would be happy as husband and wife. I'm sad about losing our home, too.'

'So am I.' She paused. 'Maybe you'll find someone to marry at the ashram.'

'Who could be as wonderful as Urmila? I would like to fulfil my duty as a son, if I can, to have a chance at a good rebirth. Maybe I can come back for her somehow.'

'I won't have to marry there. I'm glad.'

He realized what should have been obvious. 'It would be impossible for you to do what marriage requires, wouldn't it? You'd have to let a man touch you.'

'I might be able to now, with Mithraba's magic, but I still don't want to. I expect to fail at that duty. Perhaps I'll be reborn as a beetle.'

'Maybe you already have been.'

Kalyani smiled slightly, as much as she ever did. She began to stroke her gharial's back with her index and middle fingers.

'Two... four... six...' she murmured.

The familiar litany brought him comfort as he turned and faced forward.

———

Kalyani counted to four thousand ninety-six, an auspicious number. She stepped off the gharial into knee-deep water and whispered her gratitude to her friend. Aruni followed her lead, climbing from his with care.

The ground rose ahead of them and became a tangle of green just beyond the riverbank. They walked up to the edge of the forest and looked back, across the river. Smoke billowed in great clouds from the far side. Small figures stood on the shore, but she couldn't tell who they were.

Next to her, Aruni frowned and moved his hand to shade his eyes. Leeches dotted his legs, fat, black oblongs. Mithraba's wings beat within her. Her brother's posture reminded her of a wounded animal, and Kalyani reached out two fingers, stroking the back of his neck. Light seeped from her skin into his. The corpulent worms fell from her brother and crawled away.

Aruni sighed. With Mithraba's help, she knew it was good.

They turned east, toward Prayag, and walked. The city's jewelled spires rose from the river's edge like one of her brother's paintings come to life. His steps whispered against the grass. *Shish. Shush.* Her ankle bells rang in answer. *Trink. Trank.*

'We can't go into Prayag with you glowing like this.'

'I don't know how to make it stop.'

'What if we cover you with mud, like you were last night?'

'Or I could wait at the edge of the forest, while you get Mother and Father.'

Aruni shook his head. 'Too dangerous.'

'Not if I make friends first.'

Mithraba drummed against her breastbone. Tawny eyes outlined by black glinted through the undergrowth. She extended a hand toward them. Light blazed from her fingertips and palms. The grass rustled and then bent as a full-grown tigress pushed her way through, exposing long whiskers and a trim of white fur backed by orange and black stripes.

Aruni hissed. She touched her other hand to his arm. A throaty rumble emerged from the tiger as it nosed her knuckles. She stroked between its ears with two fingers.

Two. Four.

'We'll wait here for you,' she told her brother. 'She'll protect me.'

Aruni placed his large hand over hers with the weight of a feather. 'I believe you.' His voice was low but steady. 'When we reach the ashram, I'd like to paint you – that is, if you don't mind.'

'I would like that.'

'I'll return soon.' The grass whispered as her brother moved away.

A Jambu tree rose from the undergrowth and cast an inviting circle of shade. Kalyani's fingers twitched. Her palms tingled. She opened her mouth and expelled a rush of air, like blowing seeds from a puff. Light floated away in a cloud of breath, her discomfort going with it. One more riddle solved. She took eight steps to the tree and sat at its base. The tiger lay across her feet. She reached up and tapped the tree with one finger, two times, for the pleasure of it.

NAVA

Three times Nava tried to change eir skin, and three times e dissolved into primordial ooze. Three times e ended as a painful mess of skeleton, flesh, nerves and silicon. After the first two failures, Maker collected Nava into a womb and rebuilt Nava to wholeness.

After the third, e regarded Nava's ravaged form and sent, 'I'm calling in your grandmaker. I'm not sure why this is so hard for you, but maybe Grandmaker will have some insight. Don't worry. You'll come into your abilities.' Maker allowed a bit of frustration to dance around the otherwise encouraging words.

Nava found Grandmaker to be at once terrifying and irresistible. Unlike Maker's sleek, cylindrical form, or Nava's default amorphous body, Grandmaker had chosen to retain aspects of eir human ancestors. Eir skin was cold metal, but e had an ovoid body, four limbs, and a spherical case for eir brain. Grandmaker manifested eyes, ears and mouth, though all three were sealed from eir journey through the vacuum of space.

As Nava watched, Grandmaker landed on the remote planetoid that e and Maker called home. Grandmaker extended collectors from eir lower limbs into the soil and, drawing out the material e needed, Grandmaker's skin transformed into silky, dark-coloured fur. Eir limbs grew longer and more pliable, and ey gathered the remains of Nava's body, cradling them and exuding calm.

'I keep failing, Grandmaker.' Nava's brain was intact enough that e could communicate electromagnetically. Nava tagged eir message with fear and sorrow, confessing what e dared not to Maker. 'I think I might be flawed. Maker believes so but won't admit it.'

'Dear child, if your maker really thought that, I wouldn't be here,' Grandmaker responded. Eir words were wrapped with comfort and confidence. 'E expects you to struggle. You're an experiment.'

'What do you think of eir chances?' Maker sent on a broadcast channel.

'I think pain is a useless and cruel remnant of our human ancestors. Even the current ones on Earth have eliminated it.' Grandmaker's words were laced with anger. 'You ask much of your children.'

'I wasn't asking about that,' Maker responded. 'You have the recordings. What might we do to help Nava accomplish a change? And don't tell me to disable eir pain receptors. I will succeed at making a child who can use pain to eir advantage.'

Grandmaker transmitted a burst of irritation-laden static. 'We should design our children with less stubbornness. Nava, you will try again and let me observe you in person.'

E deposited Nava into the womb, then extruded an array of sensors and waited expectantly on the dusty surface. Maker floated nearby, watching as the planetoid spun lazily and the womb knit Nava's body back together.

———

Nava emerged, whole once again. E concentrated on the molecules of eir skin and the chemicals dancing in eir veins. Eir coprocessor worked out the equations. Nava forced the reactions that would turn worthless tissue into light-harvesting metal. Pain receptors triggered by thousands of micro-nerves sent insistent signals to Nava's organic brain. Overwhelmed, eir concentration failed. Ionic bonds failed. Molecular structures crumbled.

'I'm useless,' Nava wailed as eir body disintegrated. 'I can't even effect a simple skin change. What if I never do?'

'You must,' Maker sent. 'You will try until you succeed.'

Grandmaker expressed dissent interwoven with regret. 'If you can't control your body, Nava, you can't survive out here. The Solar System is no place for a static life form. If you fail, you'll be stripped of silicon and returned to Earth where you'll live as a human being.'

Nava shuddered. Though humans were their ancestors, e did not want to be trapped in a frail, fleshy sac for the rest of eir life.

'What if there's a mistake in my design?'

'I have not made a mistake,' Maker sent. 'Not this time.'

'Nava, you are the third iteration of this foolhardy attempt at novelty. Each maker is allowed three failed children on Earth. The planet can only sustain so many humans. If we had somewhere else, another habitable world... But we don't.'

Maker radiated determination. 'It's true, I've had two previous failures, but if you can learn to harness the pain, Nava, you'll have the reaction speed and mass to become extraordinary. You might build yourself into a planet. You could save humanity, free us of this idiotic population restriction.'

'It's not idiotic, and your dream borders on irresponsibility,' Grandmaker sent. 'Give Nava the code to disable eir pain neurons and let your child be functional!'

'No. Pain is an essential part of the design. Nava must feel it to learn how to harness it.'

'Then I can't be part of this any more.' Grandmaker's words were coloured with regret. 'I'm going in-system to the design review board and will recommend they investigate. What you do with Nava between now and then is up to you.'

Maker extruded an array of weapons, but with Grandmaker still cradling Nava's remains, the two adults were in a stand-off. After several tense minutes, Maker sent a go-ahead. Grandmaker deposited Nava's parts into the womb and departed.

Nava was rebuilt again.

On eir fifth attempt, Nava succeeded at changing eir skin. The result wasn't the light collecting cell array that e had tried for, but at least e stayed whole. Maker, however, spun with impatience.

'Nava, you have to do better, and quickly!'

'It's your fault for not designing me better. I'm flawed. I can't do this!'

'Are you giving up? Should I take you back to Earth?'

'No,' Nava sent, holding back the sulky tone from eir sending. 'I don't want to become human. I want to stay made.'

'Good. Then begin again!'

And so Nava changed, and changed, and changed some more. Pain and frustration were eir only other companions. Maker let Nava rest long enough to heal and replenish eir energy stores. Fifteen planetoid revolutions later, Nava had mastered the basics of transforming eir existing structure. Time was running out.

'You're almost ready to go off planet. The next feature is critical. You must learn to break down and integrate foreign matter with your body.'

Maker exuded encouragement, but Nava knew the truth: e was too slow, too prone to failure. E gathered the shattered pieces of eir confidence and attempted eir first collection.

Nava failed to integrate the planetoid's dust, always in novel ways, but often to the fragmentation of eir body. The pain was excruciating, the fire of electricity burning through eir nerves and circuits. Nava tried to make sense of the pain, to put the signals to use as Maker intended, but e couldn't make the connections.

'Enough, Nava. I can't go on like this,' Maker sent. Eir affect was pure sorrow. 'I'm exhausted. I can barely power the womb. My empathy levels are overloaded from your suffering.'

'That's not my fault,' Nava responded. Anger saturated the message. 'Change yourself! Turn your empathy circuits off. I know you can.'

'That's illegal. Makers would do terrible things to their children without strong empathy.'

'Then go away and leave me here!'

'And what then? When the review board hauls you back to Earth, do you think they'll be as kind as I will?'

'It should be my choice,' Nava replied, letting the full force of eir resentment through. 'It's my life.'

Maker sent a spike of exasperation.

'Three times I have tried to innovate, and three times I have failed. Will you have me humiliated further by pretending it isn't so?'

Nava stayed stubbornly silent.

'Very well. Stay here and face your fate alone!'

Maker assumed eir travel form, a perfect sphere covered in glittering solar cells, and departed without another sending.

For a time, Nava simply existed, waiting for the inevitable, but eir thoughts gradually turned. What right had Maker to inflict life upon Nava without knowing if e could succeed? And now, to be consigned to Earth and stripped of everything that made existence interesting – it was terribly unfair. Resentment built to anger and then rage.

A third option came to mind. Nava's thoughts circled the

new idea cautiously. Could e try to transform emself without guidance, taking the risk of failure alone? The womb's entry gaped like the dark maw of a hungry Earth animal, powerless without Maker. If Nava fell apart again, the board members would arrive to a mess of frozen flesh and fragmented metal. If e succeeded... Either way, e would be free from being a disappointment.

As the intention congealed, Nava blocked the taunting view of the womb. E reset eir coprocessor and focused on eir external sensors, shutting down the electromagnetic and radiative portions, leaving only chemical, tactile and pain.

Nava probed into the dust and rock below. Pain flared as e opened a port and drew in the foreign material, but this time, instead of rushing the process to minimize the sensation, Nava prolonged it. E paid attention to every bit of information and let the pain saturate eir consciousness.

The planetoid completed nearly a quarter revolution before Nava had integrated a millimetre of soil, but it held. A dazzling sense of accomplishment broke through the pain.

The stars hung overhead, beckoning.

Nava sucked in raw material. Fear evaporated with every successful gram that e absorbed. Pain and pleasure oscillated in eir brain while eir co-processor connections strengthened. At last, Nava understood what Maker had intended with this design. Pain was not to be avoided but embraced. Like every other input to eir body, pain had a purpose. Nava needed to feel it, letting the dazzlingly fast response signals connect from eir brain through eir processor circuits to eir body, forming a stable closed loop.

Nava absorbed all of the planetoid's material into eir now bloated body. E was massive, like nothing e had seen except in recordings of flawed beings. But Nava was not flawed.

Deep in the core of the planetoid, e had found enough ice, carbon and hydrogen to make emself an intricate network of pain nerves and return conduits. E had removed every delicate vestigial organ except for eir brain, which was now well protected in the centre of eir body. Layers of muscle kept Nava's structure active and prevented em from collapsing from eir own microgravity.

E broadcast a message to Maker and Grandmaker: 'I am whole. Come and see!'

Nava ejected small amounts of dust to change eir course upward, out of the plane of the planets' ecliptic, and then inward. The in-system greeting party, set on bringing a failed made-child to justice, must be on its way. As Nava accelerated, e overshot the small group of made beings.

'Never mind,' Nava beamed at them. 'Your task is obsolete.'

Maker and Grandmaker were in the group.

'Nava, my child – you are beyond amazing,' Maker sent. 'You've done everything I hoped for. Go! We will meet you near Earth.'

Earth. That was supposed to be Nava's ultimate destination. There, Nava could gather atmosphere and become a sentient vehicle for human beings, letting them escape the confines of overcrowding. But that was Maker's dream. Nava looked upward, inward, where the fury of the sun glared its challenge.

Nava sent a response: 'Dear Maker, whatever happens, I'm glad that you made me, but I don't want to exist to carry humans. Build yourself another child for that, one who's more inclined to serve. I dream of blazing glory.'

Maker and the others pulsed in confusion, but they followed Nava as e sailed past Earth and Venus and Mercury. At last, realization dawned on Maker. E sent a message with tremendous amplitude.

'Nava, no! Don't throw your life away so recklessly.'

'Why not?' Nava saturated eir words with glee. 'My life was forfeit not so long ago. Besides, weren't you reckless to make me?'

The others hung back as Nava stopped two light-seconds away from the sun. Heat turned eir outer layer into dark, dirty, molten glass. Nava put half eir attention into maintaining eir structural integrity.

'If I succeed at this,' Nava sent, 'it may be a long time before I find a way to communicate. In the meantime, I bid you all farewell.'

Maker and Grandmaker sent gentle sinusoids of love, taking Nava by surprise. After a moment, e reciprocated.

Turning eir attention back to the seething mass of the sun, Nava first turned off eir electromagnetic sensors. Tactile and chemical went next, but e kept the two most important: radiative and pain. E absorbed as much energy as e could hold before forming eir skin into the highest density e could.

Extruding a long limb, Nava made contact with the sun's plasma. Pain receptors and feedback circuitry screamed into overdrive as Nava held the gas at eir periphery. Nerves, neurons and circuits grew and adapted to the unfamiliar material.

Nava worked deliberately through shrieking alarms of pain. When the relief of success broke through, e accelerated the process until the synergy of agony and ecstasy changed eir body from solid to gaseous.

Nava plunged into the sun, taking in the layers of corona, chromosphere, photosphere, and finally the towering gas granules, learning and adapting eir body along the way. The intensity of sensation – the speed of eir responses – that allowed Nava to survive the heat and pressure as e harnessed the energy of the sun to rebuild. Hydrogen, helium, oxygen, and carbon were eir blood; fusion, eir metabolism.

When e reached a stable form, Nava penetrated to the core. There e remained. E no longer knew how much time passed by human or made-being standards, but e longed for contact. E directed what emissions e could, emitting neutrinos that wouldn't be affected by their passage through the many layers of this body.

To Nava's great surprise, e received a response, but not from eir ancestors or relatives. The response wasn't in any language that Nava understood, but it was encoded in neutrinos. The stream had a pattern. Realization dawned. Nava was not the first of eir kind.

BINARIES

YEAR 1: I come into the world wet and squalling and ordinary, born of heterosexual bio-parents.

YEAR 2: A flat photo shows me on my first birthday with a shock of red hair, wide green eyes, and an expression of distaste at the sticky white frosting on my fingers. My mother stands on one side looking not at all Jewish; my Goan, lapsed-Catholic father stands on the other.

YEAR 4: Shaya is born. I am a match to my mother's complexion, but my baby sister takes after our father. No one thinks we're siblings unless they see the fierce, protective scowl on my face when I'm allowed to hold her.

YEAR 8: I learn to ride a bicycle and write my first program. My intrepid little sister does as well, which makes me jealous, and yet I keep helping her. We fight over everything and drive our parents crazy. At night she sleeps curled up against my back.

YEAR 16: I graduate from high school and date my first

girlfriend who turns out to be a summer fling. On a hot August day, I leave the Midwest for the Northeast. Shaya sobs for ten minutes at my departure, sniffles, and then asks, 'Can I have your room?' I tell her yes. We message each other constantly while I'm away.

YEAR 32: I become a lawyer and get married to the perfect woman: a no-nonsense architect who dives off cliffs for fun. Shaya joins the U.S. Air Force and then NASA. She bumps Sally Ride to become the youngest female astronaut in space. After years of praising my choices, our mother is finally proud of my sister. Dad always liked her better than me. So do I.

YEAR 64: My third wife divorces me. She complains that I hold too much of myself back, and she's right, about all of my relationships. I decide it's better for everyone if I remain single. Shaya disappears. I should have written that first – I don't know why I didn't. She commands the first mission to Neptune, but a few wrong bits send them awry. The craft keeps up its ghostly pings long after the words stop coming.

YEAR 128: I replace my hands and eyes, and give up law to be an artist. I create immersives from NASA's archives, starting with the images from Neptune, and I wonder what pieces of herself Shaya would have kept. Dad died two years after she went missing. Mom lived long enough to be in the front lines for rejuv, and now she's a successful investment banker. She kept her silver hair and wrinkles. I didn't. We stop receiving pings from the ship. The void has cut off our last tie to Shaya, and I feel like I, too, am unmoored.

YEAR 256: I have almost no money left, and my pride won't let me accept any from Mom. She's one of the wealthiest people still on Earth. I sign a long-term contract with a mining corporation. They rebuild me piece by piece until I look like a trash container with too many arms. My new body is hideously ugly. It's also impervious to radiation and efficient at extracting ore from space rocks. In the back of my mind is a stray thought: Perhaps I will find some clue to the whereabouts of my sister and her ship. The trail of crumbs is stale, thought: If only my memories would fade like they used to.

YEAR 512: My contract ends. For years, I didn't eat, sleep, or piss. I mated to a docking berth, plugged in, lubricated my seals, and swapped memories of being human with my fellow miners. My mother has nebulized in the meantime. 'I'll pay you to join me,' she offers, but I decline. I spend a few months reacquainting myself with the sensations of smell, taste and skin. When the novelty wears off, I accept her offer. I discover the intoxicating world of aphysical existence, dancing through nebulas and dining on virtual champagne and caviar. It's better than the real thing. I commission a simulacrum of Shaya; she's nothing like the real thing.

YEAR 1024: I leave the solar system. A snapshot of myself is archived on Earth, and Mom has beamed out a couple of centuries ago like others who tired of consciousness. They ride electromagnetic waves and gravitational beams, hoping another life form will find them and recreate them. She left me her fortune. I used the money to build a near light-speed ship, the first of its kind, and encode myself into its every aspect. I travel far beyond the populated edges of our system, searching every possible trajectory until I find it. Then I carefully attach the ship to my hull, download a piece of myself into a droid, and go aboard. An undisturbed layer of dust coats each crewmember's final resting place. The captain's pin marks Shaya's. I'm not sure what to do or where to go next. For now, though, I am content to drift onward as we are, her back curled up against mine.

THE EGG

In the corner of the night-darkened room, tucked next to the sofa, the Egg rested on its pedestal like a modern sculpture. Its quiet hum was the only sound in the apartment; its green indicator the only light. The screen on the front of the ovoid was dark, not revealing the partially formed creature incubating within.

That wasn't right. The screen had never once been off, not while *she* had been here. She was gone now. She had slipped away quietly, without fuss, much as she'd lived.

'Promise,' she had demanded, her voice raspy, as the smells of disinfectant and rot permeated his pores. 'Promise that you'll keep it going.'

'I promise,' he'd lied. 'Don't worry.' He clutched the pills in his pocket with one hand.

In the end, she had been reduced to skin and bones. Her hand, clasping his, was a papery claw. She had always been scrawny. He'd called her chicken legs when they first met, and she'd retorted with 'stupid head'. Insults had never been her strong point. They were six years old. Love came years later, and the cancer not long after that.

She was cured the first time. A designer molecule flooded her system, keeping the traitorous cells at bay.

'Let's have a baby,' she said when hope was allowed back into their house.

'Let's have two,' he responded, and they grinned like fools and got started.

They found out not long afterwards that the molecule that kept her alive was poison to any foetus. They spent the remainder of his inheritance on the Egg – and the hormones and extractions and fertilizations.

'It will be every bit your baby,' promised the specialists.

She let them record her heartbeat and intestinal sounds for playback. The two of them used the microphone daily to stimulate budding ear drums. She sang her favourite songs in her off-key shower voice. He played his guitar and read cooking magazines aloud. They stared at the screen in fascination, watching it transform from a tadpole to an alien. The sofa seat nearest the Egg turned into a sinkhole.

The second cancer snuck in, quiet and efficient, while they were busy looking the other way. She needed another designer molecule, but she was too far down the queue. The money that would have bought her way higher was gone, so the doctors tried the old-fashioned poisons. She lost her strength, the contents of her stomach and every hair on her body, but she didn't miss a day singing to the Egg.

Watching her reclining against the cylindrical pedestal, forehead resting on the warm ovoid above, he loved her even more.

'You're beautiful,' he said.

She grinned, all teeth in a skeletal face. 'You've never lied to me before.'

'And I'm not lying now.'

The second cancer took her swiftly. The apartment looked just as it had when they'd left for the hospital two days ago, but nothing was the same. The faint glow of city lights bled around the curtain edges, painting the room in a monochromatic palette. The Egg glinted, beckoning him. He shuffled towards it slowly like an old man and tripped on the edge of the rug – the rug that they'd chosen together to cushion tender baby feet and dimpled knees.

With a trembling hand he reached out and turned on the screen. It almost looked human now, although the head was too large and the body too skinny, sort of like she had looked in those last days of life. His hand moved of its own accord, navigating the menu screens, delving deep to find that buried option that came with every Egg. His fingers hovered over the number pad.

'I'm sorry, little one,' he whispered. 'This isn't how the road was supposed to go. I wish – if only –' He sighed. 'I can't do this alone, and there's no one left for you but me, a poor excuse for a father.' He drew his hand back. 'Wait. Let's go together. I can do that much for you.'

He stood and walked to the kitchen. His steps felt lighter now that the decision was made. He filled a glass with water, just enough to swallow a few pills. As he walked the scant distance back to the Egg, he reached into his pocket and retrieved the tablets. Their small white forms gleamed like pearls in his palm.

He reclined against the Egg, as she had, and closed his eyes. *You've never lied to me before.* Her words rattled like marbles in his skull. An involuntary tear traced its way down the contours of his face. It was the pinhole in the dam, and he felt all his grief push against it and then break through.

The sobs crashed over him in great waves, and he wrapped his arms around the warm Egg, clinging to it like it were a buoy in a storm. The glass and pills fell from his hands, forgotten in the tempest. An eternity passed before he went limp with exhaustion and fell asleep, his body curled around the Egg's pedestal. The menu system quietly and automatically exited to the start, and the screen went black.

DUSTY OLD THINGS

The analog wall clock in the garage had been stuck at 3.14 for two weeks. I noticed it every day while I exercised, amused at the perennial pi-time, but I put off changing the battery. My boring suburban family life kept me busy enough that I avoided drudgery as much as possible.

Our garage bore witness to this. We hadn't moved in two decades, and things had piled up. It was a repository of disused clutter and forgotten relics. The kids were teenagers. I'd hung on to their baby items – you know, just in case. Old toys and knick-knacks with no place sat in faded plastic bins for so long that I no longer saw them.

But when the clock started running again, I noticed.

'Thanks for changing the clock battery, hon,' I said to my husband.

Travis looked at me blankly.

'The one in the garage?' I prompted.

'I didn't do it.'

'Huh. Maybe one of the kids?'

He raised a sceptical eyebrow.

'Stranger things have happened.'

The next day, the garage door opener didn't work. I pressed the button on the remote half a dozen times, banged it, shook it, and cursed under my breath.

'Mom!' admonished Mohan, my thirteen-year-old son.

'Sorry.'

'I think it needs a new battery,' said the boy genius.

It must be a natural law that all batteries in the house fail within the same month.

But a new battery didn't fix the remote.

I didn't gloat to my kid, though I was tempted. Instead, I opened up the remote and the controller and realized the codes didn't match. That should've been a red flag, but my daughter was in the middle of college applications, my husband was travelling for work, and I had too much on my mind to think deeply about a garage door opener.

The day after that, my long-broken bike computer mysteriously fixed itself. And the following day, the garage remote control switches changed again. The next morning, after getting down from my fully functional exercise bike, I checked the remote's code: different once more.

I frowned at it. Shook it around. Examined it from various angles. None provided an explanation for how they'd changed. Maybe one of my kids was messing with me. Or trying to send me secret messages. They did enjoy that kind of game, though I thought they'd outgrown it.

To play along, I wrote down the codes. I did this every morning thereafter, and nothing strange happened again, but nor could I crack the cipher. For the next few weeks, I spent my lunch breaks trying every decryption, decoding and demodulation algorithm I knew, determined not to let my children outsmart me.

My background in satellite communications led me to consider (and dismiss) many tangled, complicated systems, but the solution turned out to be simple: ASCII, as familiar to me as the back of my hand.

At the end of thirty days, I had collected this sequence: hindthejuniperhedgebehindthe. Over the next week, I realized that the pattern kept repeating as a twenty-four-character sentence. It spelled out: 'behind the juniper hedge'.

I flashed back to myself, age six, new to school and desperately needing to pee during recess. I didn't know what we were allowed to do, so I snuck behind a row of juniper bushes, squatted down, and urinated all over my brand-new shoes. My Mother noticed the yellow stains and was furious. I was humiliated as only a six-year-old can be. I had never told my husband, much less my children, this story. In fact, other than my deceased mother, no one knew.

What the hell was going on? I didn't believe in ghosts, but I did believe in science. Was there a way to communicate back to whatever – or whomever – had sent me this message?

In a communication medium, you can have two one-way channels, or you can share a two-way channel. The latter is more error-prone, so I opted for the former. I needed to find a way to signal the other side.

The next morning, feeling terrified and slightly foolish, I retrieved my daughter's toy light board from the dusty storage shelves in the garage. Amazingly, the majority of the tiny bulbs still worked. The board had a ten-by-ten grid so I could do twelve ASCII characters at a time. I spelled out, 'Is that you Mom,' and hid the board behind an empty box so my family wouldn't see it.

I couldn't focus at work that day and had an even harder time sleeping that night. Life is eventful at my age, but it's more 'Oh crap, I forgot about parent–teacher night' than 'My garage is defying the laws of nature'. I had to resist the urge to get up earlier than usual to start my workout. When I finally went into the garage, I checked the remote control switches and was disappointed to see them unchanged. Then I went over to the light board and my heart stopped. The pattern was different.

'Not Mom. Anita,' I decoded.

Anita? That was my name. My legs suddenly wouldn't hold me, and I sat on the dirty concrete floor. Future me? Past me? Parallel universe me? Any of those was better (and more plausible) than my deceased mother.

'I'm you. How?' I sent back.

I took the day off to sit and watch the board. Could we make this happen faster than once every twenty-four hours? After an hour of nothing, I was inspired by Schrödinger and put the board into the empty box. When I pulled it out, it had changed.

'You home too?' it said.

I laughed. 'Yes. Explain?'

Over the next few hours, Other-me communicated in agonizingly short bursts that she was a biophysicist and had a hypothesis she was testing — that quantum consciousness could be used to affect probability distributions across multiple universes. She was recording our exchanges as evidence.

'Why me?' I sent.

The wall clock showed me that my free time was nearly up. In another twenty minutes, I would have to leave and pick up Mohan from school. We'd go straight from there to violin practice so this would be the last light-board volley for the day.

'Not sure,' Other-me said. 'Has to be us, but of all possibles, why you? Need more study.'

———

After that one day off work, I began taking long lunch breaks to interact with Other-me. The whole thing felt too unreal to share with anyone in my world. Between my morning workouts and the afternoon sessions, I gleaned more information.

Other-me had set up her test equipment in her garage, which was very similar to mine. In spite of our professional differences, we had ended up living in the same house in the suburbs of San Jose. We had to communicate via electro-mechanical devices because semiconductors were too close to quantum effects. Apparently, she'd been trying (and failing) to send email across the multiverse for weeks until she finally figured it out.

I was planning to ask Other-me how she could send me

the designs for her equipment when we had our first hiccup. I had to work through lunch one day and couldn't tell her that I would be absent. When I got home, my daughter jumped on me to help with her calculus homework, and my son had accidentally left his cell phone in his swimsuit pocket.

I couldn't get away to check the light board until the next morning. By then, the microwave oven had conked out, half the lights in the house wouldn't turn off, and the garage clock was stuck on 3.14 again.

'Where are you?' the light board demanded.

'Busy. Stop sending!' I wrote back.

'Why?'

'Too many side effects. More later.'

Later didn't happen because I spent my lunch break getting my son a new phone. That night, after the kids were asleep, Travis and I were lying side-by-side in bed and catching up on our respective social feeds.

'I forgot to tell you,' he said casually. 'I called an electrician and made an appointment for tomorrow at ten. Everything's been so flaky lately that I'm wondering if we need new outlets or wiring or something.'

'Oh, but – I mean,' I sputtered. 'It's all working now. Again. Right?'

He looked at me sidelong. 'What's the big deal? If everything's fine, he'll tell us so, and that's that.'

'I suppose.'

'But? I'm sensing a missing "but" here.'

My brain flailed for a plausible excuse and came up empty. I put down my tablet, turned squarely towards my husband, and resolved to tell him the truth.

'Okay, honey, hear me out. This is going to sound really weird.'

By the time I finished, I thought his eyebrows were going to merge with his receding blond-grey hairline. I was tempted to post a picture of him, but then I'd have to explain to my entire friend-network why my husband looked like a demented clown.

'Do you have proof?' he demanded. 'Because if you do, we are so famous! This is going to revolutionize physics! You have to tell someone. Call Lisa! Call her now!'

'Slow down,' I said, making a calming gesture with my hands. 'It's almost midnight, and I'm not calling anyone. I haven't talked to Lisa since that alumni lecture two years ago, and I don't have her phone number anyway. I'll email her.'

He gesticulated towards my idle tablet.

'Tomorrow,' I said firmly. 'Or maybe later, after I document what's going on.'

His eyes lit up. 'That's it! You should record it as a movie.'

We stayed up whispering and speculating long after we turned out the lights. Both of us had entertained the idea of being physics majors back in college, and we remembered just enough to destroy any chance of a good night's sleep.

We woke up bleary and fuzzy-headed, and I skipped workout because I was too tired. As promised during our late-night conversation, Travis met me at the house for lunch. He had cancelled the repair appointment so the electronics in the house went haywire again. While he set up the camera on a tripod, I retrieved the light board and decoded it.

'Side effects?' it read.

'To analog electro-mech devices,' I wrote back. 'Worse when I don't read.'

'Make her spell out something longer than "rgr",' Travis said as I placed the last part of my message in the box.

The 'rgr' sequence was our shorthand for Roger, like in radio communications. I suppose we could've used the networking convection of 'ack' instead, but we were two humans and not two pieces of silicon talking.

So I sent, 'Travis is here.'

'Married?' Other-me wrote back.

'Yes. 2 kids.'

'Mohan & Steph?'

'Steph?' Travis echoed, looking over my shoulder at my decoding notes. 'That has to be short for Stephanie. Did you tell her our kids' names?'

'No,' I said, then I stared up at him. 'They must be in her universe, too. And you.' I patted his torso affectionately.

'Same kids,' I sent back.

'Theory. TTYL,' Other-me sent.

The timing worked out since Travis and I had to return to our offices. For the rest of the afternoon, my phone kept beeping with incoming text messages from my husband. Most were filled with too many exclamation points.

———

Over the weekend, Travis managed all of the kids' activities and kept them out of the house. Meanwhile, I practically lived in the garage, putting on a hat, jacket and gloves when the cold started seeping into my bones.

'Hypoth1: if sent msg is not rec'd, field effect spreads beyond intended device.'

'Fits with my observ's,' I sent back.

'Hypoth2: we are linked by locale and life.'

'Explain?'

'Locale: same house. Life: same family. But I'm divorced.'

The second idea was more difficult to test since she hadn't successfully communicated with anyone else, and as far as we knew there could be a multitude of universes where we existed. Then again, the probability of us marrying the same man, living in the same house, and having the same children seemed intuitively small.

'Will email Lisa Chan for help,' I sent, hoping that my physicist friend was a mutual acquaintance.

'No! Not her!'

Other-me definitely knew her, but the vehement objection caught me by surprise.

'Why not?'

'Same field. My discovery. Want to publish first! She could disrupt from your world. Tell no one!'

By the time I finished decoding all of that, I was annoyed at my other self and disappointed by her egotism.

'You'll still get credit,' I sent, wishing I could transmit irritation and wondering if she was feeling equally put out.

'Don't do this to me.'

I signed off then, making up some excuse to do with the kids. In truth, I felt the need for some cooling-off time before I could talk to her again. What about getting some credit for myself? I wasn't a passive participant in this discovery.

Once inside the house, I peeled off my layers and began working on our traditional Sunday dinner, pretty much the only night of the week we all ate together any more. While my hands were cooking, my mind was conjuring up elaborate, angry conversations with Other-me.

'So what's going on?' Stephanie asked that evening while we were at the table.

'What do you mean?' I said, genuinely puzzled.

'Oh, come on,' Mohan drawled. 'It's obvious.'

'What?'

'You and Dad are making some kind of movie in the garage.'

'Oh sh –'

'Mom!' said my children in unison.

I'd forgotten to hide the camera set-up. I looked desperately at Travis for an assist.

'Your mom was supposed to put the camera away, so don't ruin everything by asking questions. It's meant to be a surprise, okay? We're working really hard on this.'

His lips then quirked with the tiniest I-so-saved-your-hide smirk I had ever seen. Lucky for both of us, the kids bought it.

'I bet it's something for Christmas,' Mohan said.

Stephanie rolled her eyes. 'It's probably some awful, embarrassing family movie.'

'Chock-full of naked baby pictures,' I assured her.

———

In all my imagined confrontations with Other-me, I never came up with the one that actually ensued.

'You have family. I have work,' she wrote at our next exchange. Then she begged, 'Don't ruin my success! Aren't you happy? You don't need this. I do.'

'Yes. We're happy. But this is major! The world should know.'

'All worlds will, in time. Even yours.'

'You can't be sure.'

'Fundamental physics. Someone will figure it out. Here, it's me. Please understand?'

We left it at that for another day. I did feel sorry for my other self, but my life was so ordinary. Hers, while turbulent, was the road I hadn't taken, and look at what she was about to achieve! Then again, wasn't it enough to know that I was part of it? Even if I didn't get famous over it? I was doing mental flip-flops and feeling vaguely schizophrenic for arguing with a parallel version of myself.

Meanwhile, Travis was pushing me from the local universe. 'Did you ever hear back from Lisa?'

'Oh. Well...the thing is...I haven't actually emailed her yet.'

'What! Why not?'

'She asked me not to.'

'She? Who? Alternate-universe you?'

I nodded.

'And you'll just do whatever she tells you to?'

'No, of course not, but she's making a good case for it.'

'Which is?'

'She's divorced. She doesn't have custody of the kids, and she's dedicated her life to this project. If we get the news out here, someone on our side – like Lisa – could invent the same technology. What if they find someone to communicate with in my Other's world? Then Other-me will lose everything she's worked for.'

Travis cocked an eyebrow. 'That's a lot of conjecture.'

'Besides, we're happy here, right? We don't need all the attention a big story like this would put on our lives. Imagine the press camped out in front of our house, trying to get our pictures all the time. It'll be so disruptive, especially for the kids. Steph has college applications coming up.'

'You're the one who's always complaining about how boring our lives are. Now's your chance to change that. I can't believe you're willing to let it slip away!'

'I'm just giving her more time,' I said defensively. 'And our lives are exciting now, even if the rest of the world doesn't know about it.'

'I could do it on my own, you know? Go public. I have the movies.'

I looked at him in disbelief. 'You want us to end up divorced, too?'

'No, but you're being ridiculous,' he said, glaring at me.

'You deserve some credit for all this, and I don't understand why you won't take it.'

I didn't either, to tell the truth. He was only suggesting what I'd already thought of. Why was I defending her?

I opened my next message exchange with the question that bothered me the most.

'Divorce: why?'

'Different needs. T pushed me: do more with kids. Work less. Got resentful. You?'

'Bored. T is pushy about this.'

'Of course. He wants his way.'

That didn't entirely fit with our situation. Travis was pushing me to do something that he thought would make me happy, too.

I replied, 'We're ok. I think?'

'Don't let him force it.'

'Won't. I'm strong. You happy post-D?'

'Mostly. Love being single. Miss kids. D was rough.'

And yet our last conversation indicated that she wasn't that happy with her circumstances. Was she contrasting our lives? One of us drew fulfilment from work alone; the other had balance. We were a set of clichés. Let's hope some other versions of me were more interesting.

'Lisa?' she sent.

'I'll wait.'

'Thank you! Live for yourself, not T.'

Her words gnawed at me for the rest of the day. Would I be better off divorced, too? The thought had occurred to me before, usually in the throes of arguing over something that felt trivial after some time passed. Was Other-me a window into a possible future, or a road untravelled and undesirable?

———

I pretended to be asleep when Travis got into bed that night. He'd given me the cold shoulder all day, and the tension was making both of us sleepless. What would it be like to wake up alone in this bed? In this house? The answer laid to rest my doubts about our relationship. I'd be miserable without him.

I found Travis in the garage after dinner the next day. He was sitting near the light board with the camera at his feet. My first reaction was anger. Was he planning to make good on his threat?

Then he held up my notebook.

'You complained to her about me?'

The raw pain in his voice broke my heart.

'It's not like that.'

'Your notes tell a different story. So this is it. You want a divorce.'

I swallowed a lump in my throat. 'No! I talked to her about it because I want to save us. I don't want to split up – to be away from the kids or you – but I had to understand what went wrong.'

'You should've talked to me first. She's not you, Anita, no more than a twin would be, and I'm not him.'

He shoved the notebook at me as he went back into the house. He was right. Other-me felt like a shadow, a part of myself, but my relationship with her was still tenuous. Our bond came from the natural universe. It wasn't a choice, like my marriage was. I clutched the notebook to my chest and wiped at my tears, hoping that the kids wouldn't find me like this.

———

The tension in our household felt like cobwebs, clinging to every surface and blocking every passageway. My daughter was a basket case as college application deadlines loomed. Travis was coldly polite to me. I was guilt-ridden and withdrawn, keeping my exchanges with Other-me to the bare minimum. Poor Mohan was the only halfway cheery person, and that was because the holidays were approaching.

We finally caught a break in mid-December. Stephanie was practically dancing when she came home from school.

'I got in,' she yelled. 'Harvey Mudd gave me early decision!'

We celebrated with pizza and hot cocoa instead of our planned dinner of curried fish, rice and cauliflower. Stephanie beat an early retreat to her room to text her friends until her thumbs fell off, and Mohan went to bed with the sniffles. Travis and I found ourselves alone on the sofa at nine o'clock.

'Guess we did something right with Steph,' I said with a lopsided smile.

'Makes up for all the trouble in her first two years of school, doesn't it?'

'Honey –' I began.

'Look –' he said at the same time.

'You first,' I said, tipping my head.

He took my hand in his and sighed. 'I'm sorry, okay? I shouldn't have tried to pressure you. This is your discovery, and you should do what feels right.'

'Thank you,' I said gratefully, snuggling into him. 'I'm sorry, too, for taking our private problems to a stranger.'

He wrapped an arm around me.

'I've been thinking,' I said. 'A good compromise might be to disclose this on our end after she's published her findings – if her action doesn't ripple through to our reality somehow.'

Travis shook his head. 'Forget it. You don't have to compromise for me. I don't need to get famous, and you can have your quiet, happy little life if that's what you really want.'

'You mean that?' I sat up and looked him in the eyes. 'You're sure?'

'I do, and I am.'

Then he got up, grabbed my hand, and pulled me with him.

'Come on,' he said, leading me to the garage. 'We have a movie to make.'

We filmed ourselves saying sappy things about the kids. Later, I edited in some old footage and photos – including the promised naked baby bottoms – to make a presentable movie for our extended family gathering on New Year's Eve.

On the morning of 31 December, I was huddled in the

garage, pretending to be exercising while working the light board.

'Writing final draft. Announce on Jan 2,' she said. 'Sign off till then?'

'Yes. Alert me by switches?'

'Will do,' she promised.

I unscrewed the bulbs and put the board back into storage. As I looked around at the dusty shelves loaded down with memories, I realized just how much I appreciated having them. Lots of roads diverged in the woods of my life, but now I knew what lay around the bend of one not-taken path. I was content with my choices and my family. No matter what happened in the new year – whether we revealed our part in this grand discovery or not – my life was good.

THE BOY WHO MADE FLOWERS

When a few stray jasmine blossoms fell from Charlie Kim's ears, neither he nor his violin teacher, Mrs Janet Wong, noticed. Recitals were in three weeks, and that was their focus, especially for Charlie. The lovely Amelie would be in the audience, and he did not want to make a mistake in front of her.

Charlie furrowed his brow and bent his bow to the lilting notes of von Weber's 'Country Dance'. Yellow honeysuckle, blue asters and clusters of pink alyssum cascaded over his shoulders. Sweat, mixed with baby's breath, beaded on his forehead. Charlie was so intent on his practice that he didn't wonder at Mrs Wong's dropped jaw, nor did he marvel at the incredible scents rising around him. He finished his virtuoso performance with a flourish. That's when he saw the multicoloured blossoms surrounding his feet. He looked up, puzzled.

'They...came out of your ears,' said Mrs Wong.

'My *ears*?' Charlie squeaked.

He was breathing hard, and now his heart raced. Pure white roses and delicate Phalaenopsis sprung from his hands. Smaller blossoms continued to drop from his ears. Pink carnations caught in his throat. *This can't be happening,* Charlie thought.

'You must be manifesting,' Mrs Wong said. She frowned as Charlie coughed and shook his head. 'You'd better calm down before it gets out of hand. Take some deep breaths. I'll call your mother.'

Charlie had been waiting for most of his twelve years to discover what, if any, special ability he might have. He was hoping for something awesome so he could be like Nawemi Robinson, the war hero with fire-blasting fingers, or, at the very least, like Nawemi's wife, who could heal wounds with her touch.

Instead, as he attempted to survive carnation asphyxiation, all Charlie could think about were the tragic cases of Jasleen Banerjee – she could summon lightning, but she wasn't immune to it – and Trenton Smythe, who flew up so high and fast that he shot out to space and never returned. It would be bad enough if his ability were something floral. The idea of dying from it was mortifying. *It can't be,* Charlie thought. *Something must be wrong with me.*

His mother arrived ten minutes later. In the interval, Mrs Wong's brown and beige den had transformed into a florist's Technicolor dream.

'How beautiful,' his mother exclaimed.

Charlie burst into tears. Forget-me-nots accumulated around them in cobalt drifts.

'What's wrong with me?' he sobbed.

Charlie hadn't shown any outward signs of puberty, a known requirement for manifesting. He had yet to fill out his muscles or pop any pimples, and baby fat rounded his cheeks. The school choir director kept trying to recruit him to sing soprano.

'This can't be my ability!' Charlie's voice scraped low, confirming what the flowers had hinted at.

'Don't be silly! What else could it be? Let's pack up your violin and get you a check-up.'

———

At the clinic, Charlie was assigned to a counsellor who introduced herself as 'Miss Yaro, specialist in early-stage manifestation.'

Charlie thought she was rather pretty with her straight, chestnut-coloured hair and green eyes, though not as lovely as Amelie and far too old for his taste.

'Congratulations, Charlie! How are you feeling?'

'I'm making flowers.'

'Yes, you have an unusual talent.'

'Unusual? This is the dumbest thing I've ever heard of! I can't fight bad guys like Nawemi. I can't help sick people or fly through tornadoes. I'm useless!'

'I understand your feelings,' Miss Yaro said. 'But the fact remains, this is the ability you have. Not everyone can be a war hero. Besides, Nawemi always tells me that he hates the violence he inflicts.'

'You know him?'

Miss Yaro smiled. 'We went to school together. Now, let's start teaching you to control your manifestations.'

'Do I have to?'

'If you can't control your abilities, you could become a danger to others and yourself.'

Charlie raised a sceptical eyebrow.

'Okay, maybe not to others, but you did almost choke.'

'What about drugs to stop manifestations? I read about those when we were driving over.'

Miss Yaro shook her head. 'They're intended for extreme cases, and they come with bad side effects.'

'Like what?'

'Those drugs aren't meant for you, Charlie. Live with your ability for a while. Get to know it. You might find it easier to manage than you think.'

But Charlie was determined that he wouldn't. He let her load the edocs and videos about breathing exercises on to his phone, though he had no intention of watching them. He didn't want to meditate his way to perfect flowers. If he was cursed to have the world's most pathetic ability, he was going to make sure nobody knew about it.

That night, after Charlie ate dinner and finished his homework, his parents sat down to talk with him. This was obviously one of those conversations that deserved a Formal Title.

'So you're becoming a man,' his father said, eliciting a massive eye-roll from Charlie. 'With great power comes great responsibility.'

'Really, Dad? That's the best you've got? Besides, I don't have a great power. I make dumb girly flowers.'

'Charlie!' his mother snapped. 'There's nothing dumb about girls or flowers. That's the sort of nonsense thing my grandfather would say.'

'Well, maybe he was right,' Charlie muttered. He twitched as pale plum blossoms fell out of his ears and tickled his neck.

'Apologize to your mother, Charlie!'

'No!'

He stormed out of the room before they could say another word, afraid that his anger would manifest as a choking session. A trail of pale yellow roses dotted his wake.

Charlie kicked his bedroom door closed and glowered at the images plastered on the walls. Nawemi, Chandra, Juliette, Molten-Mike: his heroes taunted him. *You'll never be one of us.*

He vented his frustration on them, taking what satisfaction he could from the sound of tearing paper. Then he lay in bed and tried very hard not to cry.

———

Charlie woke the next day with a sense of dread. Seventh grade was hard enough without having to hide an embarrassing manifestation. At breakfast, he spat out intrusive violets between bites of toaster waffles. The smell of his father's congee and pork clashed terribly with the flavours in his mouth.

'Do I have to go?' he muttered as he dumped his dishes in the sink.

'Yes,' his mother said. 'I have three client meetings and a court appearance, and Dad's driving out to D.C. all day.'

'I could stay home alone,' he said. 'Everyone's going to make fun of me. This is the worst day of my life.'

'Don't be so dramatic! You're not sick. There's no reason for you to hide at home.'

Rain poured from clouds that hung as low as Charlie's mood. The weather prevented him from riding his bike to school so his mother drove him. Poppies and chrysanthemums littered the car interior by the time they arrived.

'Don't worry,' she said. 'You'll be fine. I'll let the school know what's going on in case you need help.'

The last thing Charlie wanted was that kind of attention. Fortunately, homeroom was incredibly boring, and first period was ancient history with Mr Kragen, whose nasal drone made it hard for anyone to stay awake. Charlie's body didn't betray him until second period.

Biology was usually his favourite subject. They had to dissect a frog, and Charlie couldn't help his revulsion at the results. That sensation expressed itself as a cascade of dark purple pansies and blue irises. He could feel the stares and questions like pinpricks on his neck. Charlie ignored them as best he could and, after class, ran-walked to the cafeteria.

His best friend was at home with the flu so he found a quiet corner to eat lunch alone. Nobody dared to harass him under the watchful eye of the monitors, but he could sense gleeful malice roaming the hall like a living creature.

The afternoon classes produced no excitement – for which Charlie was immeasurably grateful – though white baby's breath clung to his sweat during gym. By the end of the school day, the sun had broken through the rain clouds. Puddles reflected a mix of blue, white and grey. A long line of wet cars snaked through the parking lot. None of them belonged to Charlie's parents.

With a great sigh, Charlie began to walk home. He kicked irritably at the pools of water on the sidewalk, only succeeding in soaking his socks. After he turned the corner from school and went exactly two blocks, his solitude was interrupted by a shout.

'Hey! Flower Power!'

Charlie turned to see whose voice had issued the greeting. He had to swallow a lump in his throat – one that tasted suspiciously like carnations – before he had the nerve to meet his greeter's gaze. Trembling forget-me-nots fell around him.

The voice belonged to Jesse, a boy who looked more like a man than a thirteen-year-old had any right to. Two girls and three boys flanked him, all of them older and larger than Charlie.

'Look! He's doing it right now,' said one of Jesse's crew.

Charlie ran.

He made it half a block before he was jerked to a halt from behind. Multiple hands grabbed his arms and forced him against a hedge of hawthorn. The hedge stood several heads higher than Charlie's, blocking any chance of escape unless he mutated into being able to fly. Or jump really high. *If only*, Charlie thought as thorns and twigs prodded him.

'Freak him out!'

A fist ploughed into his stomach.

'Here it comes. Look out for flowers!'

Raucous laughter accompanied kicks to his shin.

'You gonna hurt us with those pretty petals?'

In between blows, Charlie watched as they dumped out and trampled the contents of his backpack. He used every ounce of willpower to wear his stoic-face. His father had told him never to cry in front of bullies, and he didn't.

Multi-coloured blossoms, crushed and fragrant, betrayed his true feelings.

'Hey, do you think they come out of his butthole?'

They forced him to turn around. Charlie ducked his head so the brambles wouldn't scratch his eyes. Someone yanked his pants down to his knees. The autumn air chilled his backside through his thin briefs. He clenched those muscles like his life depended on it.

'Aw, he doesn't crap roses. Too bad, flower boy. That might've made us like you.'

The hard grips released and giggles faded, but Charlie stood facing into the hedge. He trembled, waiting for the next act of humiliation. When, after several minutes, none came, he pulled his pants up and turned to collect his things. His face and arms stung with scratches.

He shook off the last of the roses from his palms and picked up his phone. The screen had a starburst crack in one corner, but it still worked. He called Miss Yaro.

'You have to get me those drugs!' His voice cracked midway through the sentence.

'...Charlie?'

'I got attacked by a bunch of kids because I manifested at school. Please, Miss Yaro! I want it to stop.'

'Okay, slow down. Are you hurt?'

'Not really.'

'And who did this?'

Charlie hesitated. If he had pictures or video, Jesse and his crew would be in hot water for bullying, but words weren't enough and tattling would only encourage them.

'Some kids in another grade. I don't know them.'

'I'm sorry you were attacked, Charlie, but you need to report this to your school and let them handle it. In the meantime, keep doing your exercises. You'll learn to stop manifesting, I promise.'

———

Fair weather returned the next day, and Charlie rode his bike to school unharmed. His ride home, however, was less peaceful. A branch cracked, splintering as it passed through a wheel. Air whistled past Charlie's ears. He flew off the seat, landed on his left shoulder. His helmet hit the road with a sharp rap. Fingers dug into his armpits, dragged him to the sidewalk before he could get his bearings.

Charlie was once again crushed by a hawthorn's prickly embrace when a high, clear voice said, 'Leave him alone!'

Bodies parted, and Charlie extricated himself from the foliage. Amelie and two other girls looked on from down the sidewalk, their phones positioned for good camera views. Charlie's heart sank even as he realized the benefit of their evidence.

'Did you get it?' one of Amelie's friends said.

Amelie and the other girl nodded.

'Don't send those! Please!' Jesse begged.

'We'll leave him alone,' said one of Jesse's crew. 'We swear!'

'You'd better,' said Amelie's friend.

Charlie hung his head. *Why did it have to be her?* His tormentors departed. He knelt and busied himself by gathering his school things. Golden poppies mixed with baby's breath from his sweaty palms. He wiped them on the soggy grass. Girlish whispers floated to his ears, which were a bright shade of crimson, matching the columbines emerging thence.

Charlie kept his gaze downward until a shadow fell over him. He fell back, startled, and once again displaced contents of his backpack.

'Sorry,' Amelie said and bent down to help.

'Not your fault,' he mumbled.

When he stood, backpack well zippered, he was surprised to see her looking nervous and sad. He had expected pity.

'I was wondering,' Amelie said, 'if you could help me.'

She flushed. The rosiness of her chubby, dimpled cheeks only deepened Charlie's confusion. Her words penetrated the fog in his brain.

'Of course. Anything! Do you need help with the algebra homework this week? The equations are pretty tricky.'

Amelie laughed. Charlie's spirits lifted at the sound. The heady scent of hyacinth rose around them.

'I'm already done with that. It's not a school thing.'

'Oh. I mean – I wasn't – I know you're smart. Smarter than me, for sure.' Charlie stopped stumbling over words and blew out a deep breath. 'Sorry. What do you need help with?'

Amelie's flush deepened. Her eyes glistened with tears.

'It's your flowers. My granddad died a few days ago, and his funeral is coming up, and he really loved his rose bushes. I want to cover his coffin with white roses, but his plants are almost bare. My mom says it's too expensive to buy that many. I saw what you can do. I thought maybe you could make them for me, for the funeral.'

'Yes,' said Charlie. 'Sure. Of course.'

'The service is on Saturday. Could you come early in the morning and do it? So they're fresh?'

Charlie bobbed his head in the affirmative. He didn't stop to wonder how, with no control over his abilities, he would fulfil Amelie's wishes. At that moment, watching her face light up with relief, he couldn't think of anything but her happiness.

'Thanks, Charlie! You're the best!' She grabbed her phone. 'What's your number? I'll text you the address.'

The digits stumbled from Charlie's brain to his mouth in the correct order. She gave his hand a strong squeeze, then ran off to join her friends who waited down the block. Charlie righted his bike and rode home in a blissful daze.

It wasn't until he was reading his English assignment that Charlie realized he had no idea how to make roses happen. Homework forgotten, he dialled Miss Yaro who answered immediately.

'Charlie! Are you all right?'

'Sort of.'

She sighed. 'Perhaps I should talk to your school administration myself.'

'No. I'm not calling about that.'

'Then what's the emergency?'

'I need to know how to make roses.'

Baffled silence emanated from the phone. 'Tell me what's going on.'

'I told a friend I could make them for her. I mean, not her, but for her grandpa. For his funeral. It's in a few days. I really need to learn how to make white roses before then.'

'Oh, Charlie, what a lovely thing to do. I'd be glad to help if I can. My best guess is that the type of flower is tied to emotion. Manifestation seems related to the endocrine system, which is why hormonal changes for puberty are usually the first trigger.'

'But what does that mean?'

'It means you need to keep track of what you're feeling and what your body is doing, and which flowers go with those sensations.'

'I'm not really good with feelings.'

'Everybody is good with feelings,' Miss Yaro said. 'Because everybody has them. As an almost teenager, your emotions may be complicated and changeable, but you'll figure them out once you pay attention.'

That night, Charlie finished his homework in record time and retired to his room without watching any television shows. When his father came up to say goodnight, he discovered his son in a state of red-faced exertion. Charlie's room looked like a floral typhoon had passed through. Crushed petals and buds littered every surface, mingling with the torn-up posters from two nights past.

'What is the matter, Charlie? Are you all right? Should I call Miss Yaro?'

Charlie's father had his phone in his hand, ready to dial.

'No. It's okay, Dad. I'm practising.'

'Practising? Oh. That's...good. I'm glad. Clean this mess up before your mom sees it, okay?'

Charlie nodded, and his father gave him a gentle hug.

'I'm proud of you.'

'Thanks, Dad.'

'Don't stay up too late.'

After his father left, Charlie entered the last notes of the night: 'Roses mixed in with other stuff: feeling scared, maybe? Or worried.'

———

Over the next two days, Charlie kept at his log whenever he could get to his phone. He skipped after-school soccer practice so that he could work on his manifestations. He spent half his time identifying the flowers. Botany wasn't a subject he'd paid much attention to.

Charlie discovered a strong correlation between chrysanthemums and confusion, daisies and frustration, but the connection to roses remained unclear. Roses came with fear, nervousness, worry, and any other strong reaction. Sometimes they were white. Given that he often felt scared and full of strong emotion when he was around Amelie, he hoped he would make enough by accident for the funeral.

———

Charlie woke on Saturday morning feeling plenty nervous. He swallowed pansies and violets with breakfast, then put on his soccer clothes.

'Have a good game,' his mother called as he ran out the door.

Instead of cycling to the soccer field, Charlie rode to the funeral parlour. Amelie met him at the door. She wore a black knee-length dress with her dark hair swept back by a matching headband. Charlie glanced down at his bright blue-and-green soccer uniform.

'Sorry about the outfit,' he said, wishing he'd thought to bring a sober change of clothing. 'I kind of didn't tell my parents I was coming here.'

'That's okay. Come on back.'

She led the way to a plain oak casket. It rested in a room that was decorated with some sparse flower arrangements and an old brown sofa. Charlie gazed at Amelie's puffy, tear-streaked face and let his emotions loose. Fear and nervous energy tied his stomach in knots. Poppies, mums and roses tumbled out of him.

He frowned at the blooms and concentrated. Jasmine mingled with the others. What was he afraid of? Disappointing Amelie. He focused on wanting to make her happy, and the roses vanished. He focused on his fear of failure; that didn't work either.

Then he imagined succeeding. His heart raced and he felt flutters in his stomach. He pictured his triumph and her winning smile, perhaps a hug...or even a kiss? Pristine white rosebuds fell from his hands. *Aha!* He held out his arms, closed his eyes, and held to the nerve-wracking idea of success.

Roses poured from his hands. They came as buds, full blooms and half-opened blossoms like Amelie's parted lips. Though mostly white, some were blush pink (he liked her) and pale yellow (he was concerned for her). If Charlie's eyes had been open, he would have seen Amelie's sadness lift and be replaced by wonder.

When the mound of flowers tickled Charlie's ankles, Amelie said softly, 'I think that's enough.'

Charlie opened his eyes and looked around. He frowned. 'Oh, no! I'm sorry.'

'What! Why?'

'So many of them aren't white. I'll sort them out.'

'Never mind, Charlie. They're perfect! I know Granddad would love them. Thank you so much.'

Amelie gave him a light hug, grazing him with her warmth. She scooped up an armful of roses and scattered them on the coffin. Charlie bent to help. His whole body trembled with relief. As he straightened, their eyes met, and they smiled.

'I wasn't sure I could do it,' he confessed. 'I'm not very good at this yet.'

'Are you kidding? That was amazing. You're going to make so many people happy.'

'I...I am?'

'Duh, Charlie. People love flowers.'

That was true. Maybe his ability wasn't quite as useless as he feared. If it could make Amelie happy, it couldn't be all that bad.

As they placed the last of the roses on the casket, a middle-aged man dressed in a black suit entered the room. His resemblance to Amelie was unmistakable.

'What's all this?'

'Dad, this is my friend Charlie, from school.'

'Nice to meet you,' said Amelie's father, sounding distracted. 'Amelie, where did you get all these roses? I thought Mom talked to you about this.'

'Charlie made them.'

Charlie's nervousness in front of Amelie's father demonstrated his abilities. More roses fell, though this time they mixed with columbines from his reddened ears. The manifestations stopped after Amelie's father smiled.

'Now I understand. I've never heard of someone who can make flowers. My father would've been envious.' He clapped Charlie on the shoulder. 'You've been very kind to help Amelie like this, but I'm afraid it's almost time for the service.'

Charlie nodded. *Time to go.* His tongue felt glued down, and he hurried out. He was halfway to the soccer field before he realized he hadn't said goodbye.

————

Two weeks later, Charlie Kim walked on to a small stage with roses and yellow-purple pansies trailing behind him. He had learned how to stop his manifestations in most situations, but the recital was too overwhelming to worry about a few stray blossoms.

Rows of white folding chairs lined the community centre auditorium, filled by students and their families. On stage, Mrs Wong sat at a grand piano, waiting to accompany him.

Charlie wore his only suit for the occasion. A single white rose peeked from the buttonhole. He took his position and bowed. Tucking his violin into place, he closed his eyes, breathed deeply twice, and played.

The opening triplets of von Weber's 'Country Dance' traipsed through the hall. Jasmine and alyssum drifted to the stage as Charlie concentrated on the rising and falling tones, on the pairing of bow and string. This time, he was well aware of the posies around him, but he ignored them.

When he finished – with only a few missed notes – polite applause rose from the audience. Charlie spotted his parents clapping enthusiastically. He smiled at them. Then he saw Miss Yaro standing in the back with none other than Nawemi Robinson. Nawemi winked and gave him a thumbs up. Charlie grinned so wide that his cheeks hurt, but he kept scanning the audience until he found *her*.

Amelie sat in the second row with some other students. She beamed at Charlie. He put down his instrument – gently, under Mrs Wong's sharp gaze – and scooped up the fragrant blossoms around him. He flung them over the audience, bringing forth an eruption of cheers. He felt exactly like a hero.

SHIPS IN THE NIGHT

The problem with seeing the future is that you can do nothing to change it. Kuni had figured this out long ago, when she was still a young child. People would ignore you, disbelieve you, or resent you. After enough failed attempts to change the course of events, she stopped trying.

This made it no easier for her to go about her life. She gained and lost friends, failed exams, fell in love, and had her heart broken. When she went to college and majored in physics, she felt the mathematical beauty of her foresight for the first time. Of course she couldn't change the future. Time was an illusory concept. Everything that was going to happen had already happened, and she was simply another node in the fabric of the universe – along for the ride but with an extra-dimensional view.

The realization led Kuni to change her major to philosophy, and she went on to form her doctoral thesis around the subject. Naturally, this came as no surprise to her.

When Kuni was twenty-seven years old, in the midst of writing her dissertation, she met Isra. Isra was gorgeous:

petite, curvaceous, dark hair, thick lashes and deep brown eyes that were almost black. She was also like Kuni's favourite rock.

Throughout Kuni's life, she had found comfort from objects that changed little through time. The oak tree in her parents' backyard was one. The granite boulder in her grandparents' Kyoto garden was another. The boulder was particularly soothing since it was effectively unchanged on the timescale of Kuni's life. It was a relief for her to cling to its rough surface and let that part of her mind rest.

Isra was like that rock.

Kuni had seen her many times at the Koffee Klatch, where Isra worked. She had foreseen their failed, short-lived relationship, but a silent movie of her own future told her little about the other woman's life.

The first time they touched, hands brushing as Isra handed her a mug of hot chocolate, she saw Isra's future: an unending sameness. Not literally, of course. Isra lived, breathed, moved, took coffee orders and wiped tables. She went home, had lovers (there was Kuni herself), moved to other towns. But she never changed.

Kuni stood at the pick-up counter, steaming drink in hand, and hoped Isra couldn't see the shock on her face.

'Hi, I'm Kuni,' she blurted, trying to cover her confusion.

'What an interesting name,' Isra said politely. 'Where is it from?'

'It's Japanese, short for Kuniko.'

'You don't look Japanese,' Isra said. Her smile took the sting from the comment.

'My dad's from Japan. Mom's Ethiopian. Everyone says I look more like her.'

Isra shrugged. 'Either way, I think you're beautiful.'

A few days later when the moment and the memory aligned, Kuni asked her out, and Isra accepted. They first kissed under a full moon. Isra's lips tasted like cardamom and coffee. Kuni was intoxicated and utterly at peace as she held Isra in her arms.

For two weeks, Kuni enjoyed the romance and avoided the questions, but then it was time. She held Isra's hand as they meandered through the arboretum. Sunlight speckled the ground around them, and the breeze carried the astringent scent of eucalyptus. Birds chittered, and leaves rustled, but they were otherwise alone. No human ears would be privy to this conversation.

'What are you?' Kuni asked.

'What do you mean?' Isra said, sounding puzzled.

Kuni stopped walking, not letting go of the warm fingers entwined with her own, and forced Isra to a halt.

'You never change. You never age, or grow fatter or thinner. You never have a grey hair. You just go on and on and on.' Kuni's voice faded as she drifted into the bliss of timelessness. 'It's wonderful.'

Surprise. Suspicion. Doubt. Fear.

Isra had an expressive face.

'How do you know?' she whispered, fingers tightening painfully.

Kuni took a deep breath and said the words aloud for the

first time in her life. 'I can see the future of anything – or anyone – I touch.'

Isra stared at her for a moment and then demanded, 'So tell me when mine will end!'

'I don't know,' Kuni said, taken aback. 'I can't see past my own death.'

'You're lying! You're going to kill me!'

'What? No. Don't be crazy. I could never –'

'Please!' Isra released Kuni's hand and grabbed her by the shoulders. 'Just do it!' she said, shaking Kuni with all her tiny might.

She prised Isra's hands away as gently as she could. 'I'm sorry.'

Tears pooled in two sets of dark eyes.

'Go to hell!'

'Why?' Kuni said, her voice raw.

'You really have to ask? I've been alive so long, I can't even remember how I got this way. I'm tired. So incredibly tired.'

'I'm sorry,' Kuni said again. 'I wish there was another way I could help. Stay with me,' she pleaded, ignoring the part of her brain that told her the truth, that she would never see Isra again. 'Maybe I can make it better – somehow.'

Isra sighed. The desperate anger in her face melted into desolation. 'You'd be the worst of all. With anyone else, I can fake it. Have a fight, leave, start over. I can pretend to be someone new. I'm even good at lying to myself, but with you? I'd have to face the truth. Every time I looked at you, touched you – no. I can't do it. Goodbye, Kuni.'

Isra stood up on her toes and kissed Kuni with a slow,

lingering touch of lips on cheek. Kuni's heart ached. She had seen this moment, knew it would come, but it still hurt.

When Isra had gone, Kuni walked over to the pond and found her favourite stone. The great grey slab jutted over the murky water, and she lay down on its sun-warmed surface. For once, she didn't care who saw her or what they thought. For once, life had surprised her, just a little bit, and she held tightly to that feeling. She closed her eyes, breathed deeply, and imagined the aroma of cardamom and coffee.

GAPS OF JOY, AND A KNOT FOR LOVE

Prakash's wife lay on a mattress as old as their marriage and as sunken as her cheeks. Devi's hair was grey like the threadbare curtains, her body swollen and sweaty with betrayal, consuming itself in an immunological civil war. The doctor had shrugged in apology and prescribed pain medicine. 'Nothing else we can do,' he'd said and left.

Their careworn daughter stood beside the bed. They'd named her Khushi – happiness – and Prakash's magic had kept her true to her name until Devi became ill. Shadows crowded the space under Khushi's eyes. Lines furrowed in her skin with a depth that belonged to someone older, someone like her father. She clutched an empty plastic bottle.

'We have no money left for more pills,' she whispered over her mother's ragged snores.

'How much rice do we have?'

'Enough for two days, but we've nearly run out of milk.'

'I'll go to the parks today. It's only Wednesday, but perhaps a few families will be there.'

Prakash felt for his last pocket of happiness and blew a soft breath at his wife. Her breathing quieted. Not as effective as drugs, but better than nothing. Khushi watched and shuddered – the tension of an addict in withdrawal.

Guilt stabbed at Prakash. Months had passed since he had enough joy to share with Khushi. His daughter's work as a cook paid their bills. His tips from bubble-blowing earned enough to pay for their grains. Their happiness, however, could not be resupplied with money.

He left the room and gathered his supplies: a bottle of water, a jug of soapy solution, and a thin white towel. Outside, a light breeze pushed against sultry air of Tiruchi. A crack in the middle of Prakash's sandal dug into his foot as he hobbled over uneven roads. Autorickshaws honked and careened past him, while the two-wheelers let their motors do the talking: 'Move over, old man, lest we crush your feet!'

He paused at his usual turn. To the right lay the wealthier neighbourhoods with their manicured parks and children in Western clothes and parents who dropped generous bills at his feet. The children shrieked in delight at his handiwork, but the air of adult suspicion – never trust an old man in rags – tainted their joy.

Two days' worth of rice, Khushi had said. The strain on her face gnawed at his resolve. Turn left today? To the shanties? The good parks would be mostly empty until the weekend, three days away. They could make the food stretch until then.

Prakash turned left towards the shanties where he grew up, the neighbourhoods he'd neglected since his wife took ill. He knew he was close when he could smell the sewage and rotting food. He filled his lungs. Best to get it over with. The sound of young voices – calling, laughing, exclaiming – reached him next. He rounded the corner.

Barefoot boys with skin the colour of sandalwood and eyes like night played a riotous game of cricket. Their field was dirt, broken bricks, cement rubble. Bits of plastic littered the uneven surface like dusty jewels.

'Bubble Thatha!'

They called him Grandfather, though he had no grandchildren of his own. Not yet, but when – if – Khushi had children, they would inherit his magic.

'Stop the game!'

'He's back!'

At their cries, girls emerged from tin-shanty doors like shy butterflies, strands of jasmine woven through their braids and black paste marking their foreheads with perfect, tiny dots. They threaded into the cluster of boys, their faces alight with sunshine and bright expectation.

Warm air stirred as Prakash took his first gulp of soap solution. He closed his eyes, found the hard knot of love nestled between his heart and stomach, used it to push the solution through his lungs, into his mouth, and out, out and away, between lips forming an 'O' of wonder.

The first outpouring was a cluster of small but multitudinous bubbles, at least one for each child to catch. The girls and boys shrieked, leaping about like cubs chasing after birds. Prakash inhaled their unadulterated joy. It flew to him on currents of air. He drew it through his lungs and beyond, to the interstices of his abdomen where laughter liked to live.

He took more time with the next round. He sent forth great oblong shapes, longer than any child was tall and fatter by a wide margin. The younger ones watched in awe as the prodigious forms swirled with every colour of the rainbow. The older ones jumped and tried to pop the bubbles' undulating bellies. They got all but one. It floated away, over rooftops of thatch and cement, disappearing into the aquamarine sky.

'More, Thatha, more!'

Their eagerness nestled into the warmth of his gut. He drew on the gentle possessiveness this instilled and shaped his cheeks and tongue and lips to produce a menagerie of soapy air. Rabbits, lions, giraffes, deer, and the more familiar – cows, goats, chickens – drifted over the lot like delicate blown glass.

A tendril of disappointment stole into him with the next indrawn breath. A young girl wearing peacock green stood to one side, frustration painting her face. She was new to him. He beckoned her over.

'What's the matter?' he said.

'I can't catch any of them! I run fast, but I always miss.'

'Try standing still. Let the bubble find you, and then chase it.'

She returned to her spot, scepticism in her posture. The joy he gathered was precious, but he spent a pinch to infuse the peacock-shaped bubble that floated her way. Her doubt made way for wonder. The happiness she exuded more than made up for what he'd lost, and his insides swelled.

Clouds blew in on the next breeze, casting shadows and dulling the shine on Prakash's creations. Afternoon thunder rumbled in the distance. The children groaned as one. They knew that the show was over, and they murmured their thanks as they drifted home.

'Will you come again?' asked the peacock girl.

He rinsed his mouth with water, wiped it clean with the towel, then spoke: 'Tomorrow, and every day but Saturday.'

'Why not Saturday?'

'Because I get more happiness here than anywhere else, but I am still human. I need to make money to feed my family.'

The first heavy drops landed. The daily downpour followed within minutes. Prakash's leather sandals became waterlogged and slippery with mud. The knot of love below his heart felt loose, ragged, but joy rumbled and quivered in his abdomen. It begged so hard for release – *let me help you!* – that he capitulated. He had plenty to spare today.

The house smelled of boiled milk and steamed rice, simple food for strained constitutions. Prakash dried off and went to the bedroom. Khushi lay beside her mother, the lines of strain eased by sleep. As he gazed at them, love gathered the frayed edges of the knot below his heart.

He sat on the chair next to his wife and took her hand.

'You're here,' Devi whispered without opening her eyes.

'Yes.'

Prakash inhaled, drew joy from deep in his belly, and blew the infused mist towards his wife's face. Her breath grew more even. A touch of colour returned to her skin. The corners of her lips tipped upward in a gentle curve like the base of a bubble.

'It's better than the medicine,' she murmured, passing into her dreams once more.

Khushi stirred, opened her eyes, and sat up.

'Did you bring milk? I'll start on dinner.'

She rose and walked towards the door.

'Wait,' Prakash said. 'I didn't get any milk, or money.'

'But – I don't understand.'

'Forgive me. I think we need comfort even more.'

He placed his hand on Khushi's head as if to bless her. Bubbles the size of champagne effervescence passed between them, and a sigh escaped her lips. Her frown eased. Her shoulders lifted. Her smile reflected her name.

'Thank you, Appa. I'll cook some rice, just enough for Amma, none for you or me.'

Khushi's gaunt figure left the room. Prakash returned to his bedside vigil, ignoring the hunger cramps in his stomach, exhaling well-being, and inhaling the love that saturated their home. Little by little, he repaired the frayed knot below his heart. By morning, the gaps in his belly would be empty, but his love perfect.

STRANGE ATTRACTORS

The first time, we stayed together for fifty years. The divorce was my doing. I fell apart a few months after we received our permanent extensions, at a hotel on Nassau, the same one where we'd taken our honeymoon. We were sitting side by side on a balcony, basking in the sun and the moist, salt tinged air.

'We're truly forever now,' I said, fixing my gaze on the hazy blue horizon and not his face. 'What if this isn't right? What if there's another woman out there who'd make you happier?'

'Not this again,' he groaned. 'After all these years, how can you be so insecure?'

'Wrong answer,' I said. 'If you'd told me that I'm the only one you'd ever want, I would have believed you.'

I walked out of that room and refused to see him again, not even to serve the documents.

———

We were apart for nearly a decade before we both decided that we were better with each other than anyone else.

'Should we, maybe, have kids?' he said tentatively as we laid in bed on our second honeymoon. His pale skin glowed in the moonlight, and his copper hair sparkled and curled around my dark fingers.

I looked up into his clear hazel eyes. 'I think I'd like that. How about we start tomorrow?'

He laughed, a deep, drum-like thrum which always made me warm inside. 'Sure, why not?' He planted a kiss on my nose. 'I love that you can still surprise me.'

We raised three children and stayed together for sixty-two more years. That sounds like a lot of progeny to spawn in a few decades, but we really wanted to travel, and once we were off Earth that avenue would be closed. We waited until the kids were grown and settled, or as settled as a person can be with a scant thirty years of experience, and then had nearly two blissful decades of tourism around the Solar System.

Our favourite spot was Ganymede station's view lounge. We lay curled up together on a sofa watching Jupiter's psychedelic storms.

'It's utterly mesmerizing,' I said. 'Have you seen the vids of L2-Vega?'

'That reminds me, while I was at the bar, I overheard someone say that they've opened a new portal to Vega.'

'Fantastic,' I exclaimed, sitting up straight. A second portal meant the system would open to tourists. 'We could do it, you know. We have the funds now that kids aren't drawing on them.'

'We could afford it,' he said, 'but I don't know about going away for that long. The round trip time penalty is, what, around forty years? We'd miss seeing so much of the kids' lives.'

I waved my hand dismissively. 'They're adults. They should learn to be on their own. Besides, it'll be a while yet before they have the credit for babies. This is the best time to go, and our funds aren't going to be so high forever. We got lucky with the portal manufacturer we chose.'

'It wasn't luck,' he protested.

'Fine, fine, it was your skill and timing, but you haven't always struck the gold mine. Remember the ion engine flop?'

'How could I forget? You bring it up at least once every five years. Haven't I more than made up for it since then?'

'Of course,' I soothed, not mentioning the influx of credit I had brought in with my patents. 'I am so proud of what you've done, and I love you, and I think we should take advantage of our situation and see the galaxy.'

He shook his head and sent copper braids flying around his face in the low station gravity. 'I won't go,' he said, 'but I won't ask you to stay, either.'

Nothing I said would change his mind and so I blame him for our second split. I went. He stayed, the stubborn fool.

———

The third time was a couple of centuries later, and we had changed so much that we didn't recognize each other. I saw her at a portal in the Gliese system, solar wings shimmering in the starlight, hair shorn, and limbs contracted into travel buds. I was still mostly human in appearance for I'd been travelling too much to keep up with technology, but I had gone neuter-male and had added a lot of radiation protection to my organs. That had been exhilarating in so many ways until I saw her. I felt a flash of envy, but the attraction overcame it, and I struck up a conversation once she was in station.

We talked incessantly for hours, flush with early romance, and then she said, 'Let me show you my fourth-level descendants back on Earth.' She extended a biowire, but I didn't have a port. It's easy to blow your money once you leave the Milky Way.

'That's all right,' she said, smiling. She extruded a light cube and placed it in my grateful hand. I pushed it into my wrist.

'What beautiful babies,' I exclaimed as the images scrolled before my eyes. And they were indeed, all chubby and wide-eyed and adorably *Homo sapiens*. Then I saw the family portrait, four generations arranged artfully in rows – all except for their great-grandmother.

'That's – you –' I stopped, lost for words.

Her brow creased with a delicate furrow of puzzlement. I copied over a few of my own memories and passed the cube back to her. The crease disappeared, and she closed her crystalline eyes for a few eternal minutes. When they opened, they were clear hazel and glistening with tears.

'I thought you'd gone forever,' she whispered.

I smiled and leaned in for a kiss. 'Forever is a long time.'

SOFT WE WAKE

My mother's voice, soft and insistent, rouses me. 'Wake up, Hikaru.'

I open my eyes to someone who is not my mother. This thing calls herself a person, and she is human shaped, but my mind rejects the glittering skin and glassy eyes. She stands next to my bed, a simple cot framed by dark wood, set in one corner of my temporary room. A window lets in the morning light. If I stretch my arms wide, I can almost touch the walls.

'Your breakfast is ready.' She steals a voice from my past in a misguided attempt to bring comfort. 'Will you eat here or in the garden?'

The aroma of steaming rice, tamagoyaki and broiled salmon rise from the tray that it carries. My mouth waters.

'The garden,' I say and sit upright.

Metallic lips curve into a smile. 'You're feeling adventurous today. That shows progress.'

Artificial sunlight flickers through real trees that dapple shade upon the real grass. I sit alone at a wooden table. Four others remain, also sitting by themselves. Of our original seventy-five, three were unrevivable. A dozen moved out almost immediately, embracing the enhancements offered by these future humans. Others took longer. Some made the transition hand-in-hand with a loved one. Those pained me the most.

As I eat, I think of the birdsong that accompanied my childhood breakfasts in Kyoto. The silence here is discomfiting.

When I'm finished, my not-mother returns to remove the dishes. 'Would you like to begin your departure treatments today?'

'No.'

'Very well. A tour perhaps? Numbers twelve and sixty-two have expressed interest. You could join them.'

'No.'

'The counsellor advises –'

'I know. I don't care. Leave me be!'

My rudeness disturbs me. I can imagine my real mother chiding me for interrupting. My not-mother maintains her composure as always. She bows her unnatural ovoid head and departs on silent feet, politely leaving unspoken that my time here is drawing to a close. In this future-life, you can't remain old or sick or unproductive for long.

I move to a stone bench that encircles a pool of water. My fingers break the surface tension and create ripples. Fine wrinkles trace the back of my pale skin. I passed my prime before going into storage. Silver chased my black hair, and grooves decorated the corners of my eyes and mouth. Our caretakers have offered us youth. I could live a second life, but what good is that without kinship?

———

'Wake up, Hika-chan.' My father's voice is gentle but firm.

My not-father has four arms and four legs. Our caretakers change weekly. I roll over and close my eyes, but my traitorous stomach rumbles and insists that I eat. It has always been my nemesis.

After breakfast I walk by myself through hallways tiled in earthen hues: tan, grey, ochre, brick. I find myself at the door to the cryo-chamber and push it open. The rows of capsules are all empty – dusty, gunmetal coffins – and I aim for mine: number fifty-three. The cover opens with an echoing click. I climb in and lie down. The ceiling above curves in spotless white perfection.

'Do you wish you were still asleep?'

I bolt upright. My cheeks burn.

A woman with a gaunt frame stands in the doorway. The number eight is woven into her shirt and partly covered by her grey-blond braid.

'We weren't asleep. We were frozen.'

She shrugs. 'No real difference. Why haven't you left?'

I look away. 'I don't like the way they live now, so inhuman.' I cannot stop the shudder that passes through me.

'They can take those feelings away.'

'Yes. They can change us in many ways, but then what's left? Who would I be?'

She shrugs again. 'My name is Anika.'

'Hikaru. Nice to meet you,' I say out of habit. 'Sometimes I think it would be easier if they forced me out.'

'They won't. "Living must be a choice," et cetera.' She sighs. 'I wish I were dead.'

When I look at the door again, she's gone. Her Scandinavian features spark memories of my adolescence: lake-effect snow in our Rochester yard and Sunday beer runs across state lines; the pinch of a mosquito bite; the crisp-soft contradiction of fried cheese curds. When I arrived in the United States, these things were as foreign to me as I to them. But youth is elastic. It adapts in ways that an elderly mind cannot.

———

In the afternoons, I attend the mandatory counselling sessions. My therapist appears in human form – a plump and disarmingly middle-aged female of indeterminate ethnicity – but without any substance. Her figure is made of light, a projection inhabited and controlled by a remote entity whom I've never met. She has no name.

'I'm your doctor,' she said at our first meeting. During a later session, she explained that some people don't use sound or letters for their names. It's no longer polite to rely on audio speech identifiers.

I sit on a sofa decorated in tasteful earth tones with splashes of colour in the form of embroidered flowers.

'The best way to overcome your anxiety is to take small steps of exposure,' the doctor says.

'I've watched the recordings.'

'That's good. Next is to go outside the facility, experience the world from the safety of a vehicle. We can ease the discomfort if you give us permission.'

I squeeze my hands around a throw cushion. 'How can I when I hardly understand what you're planning to do? I hate making these kinds of decisions! I never had to...before. Kian was the certain one, not me, and he isn't here. Can't you decide what's best and do it? Or put me back in the freezer. I don't care.'

The doctor's image crinkles its face until it exudes sympathy.

'Change can be difficult to accept, especially for people from an era like yours. Why not give our world a try, Hikaru? Take the modifications, become a productive citizen, integrate with modern society. If you don't like it, you can elect to go back into storage after six months. Isn't it better to take that initiative than go by default?'

No, dear doctor, not for me. Far easier to freeze like the proverbial deer in headlights and let the inevitable take its course.

'Wake up, babe,' says my lover, full of promise and temptation.

'No, not that voice!'

I glare at the hovering crystal orb. My stomach churns with anger and bile.

'I apologize,' it says, switching to my grandmother's voice. 'I missed the note in your file.'

Kian was supposed to be number fifty-four, waking up by my side to a brighter future together. He convinced me to go first, after my heart attack. My technophile lover: convinced that in the future, humanity would be able to cure many medical problems. In that, he proved right.

'They'll probably print you a new heart!' he'd said. 'I can't wait to see what else they can do.'

His final kiss scraped my upper lip with stubble, assailed my nose with coffee-breath. His brown eyes crinkled with the same irrepressible enthusiasm that drew me to him.

You should be here! You promised I wouldn't have to do this alone.

They let me search their archives, but even ones and zeros are lost with enough time. If Kian left me a message – a reason why a stranger climbed out of the capsule next to mine – I couldn't find it. I wish he'd carved it in stone.

My not-grandmother escorts me to the garden, where I see Anika, alone. I approach her table.

'May I join you?'

She pulls back slightly, but she says, 'Yes.'

I raise miso soup to my lips and let the salty liquid burn my tongue and warm my belly. They will make us any food we want. I dined at a Michelin-starred restaurant with Kian for our twenty-fifth anniversary, but my cravings here are for childhood simplicity.

Anika slices sausage into delicate circles and lifts them to her mouth.

'Where did you live, before?' I ask.

'Here. I mean, what used to be here.'

The cryogenic facility had been in Stockholm, far from the fog enshrouded bays of San Francisco where my lover and I grew old together. I don't know what they call this place today, and I don't want to. We should've been restored to life long ago, but we were neglected; not forgotten, but low priority. They said a humanitarian spent years of productivity credit to bring us back. The label seemed ironic.

'Your English is very good,' I say to Anika.

'So is yours,' she says.

I incline my head. 'Point taken. I moved to the United States when I was eleven.'

'Canada for me, for work. I was a professor of chemistry.'

'The other day – you didn't say why you're still here.'

A shadow darkens her expression such that I regret asking. An apology is on the tip of my tongue, but she speaks first. 'My daughter put me in the chamber. I knew nothing about it. Dementia.'

I work to keep the surprise from showing on my face. The counsellor said they wouldn't heal my heart without my permission. They also refused to give me the medication I'd been taking before, at home.

'The pharmaceuticals of your time were barbaric,' the doctor had explained. 'A blunt instrument for a delicate problem. We have much better treatment options, but you will have to integrate yourself first.'

No, thank you, doctor. I've never been fond of machines. I used them when I had to, to sell my artwork, and I want no part of me to become artificial.

But how had Anika's mind been restored?

My expression betrays me, or perhaps she's heard the question from others, because she answers it anyway.

'They fixed my brain enough for me to function again. There are parts of my life I can't remember. Lost forever.'

'I'm sorry.'

She shrugs. 'Ironic, isn't it? Our caregivers are so concerned with choice and consent, and yet here I am because I had neither.'

I don't know how to respond to the bitterness that permeates her words so I scoop a forkful of fried egg into my mouth.

'Two more people have left the facility,' Anika says.

'Oh.' I'm grateful for the change in subject, but I wonder if I'll be the last to go. I redirect the conversation a different way. 'Whose voice did you get today?'

'My favourite uncle – my father's younger brother. He was only ten years older than me, and he understood me like no one else.' Her eyes brim with unshed tears, and she pushes her chair away from the table. 'I lost my mind before any of them died, but now...now they're all dust, and here I am.'

'I miss them, too,' I say.

My words come soft, and Anika is walking away. If she heard them, she gives no sign.

———

Our grace period at this transitory home dwindles to four days. Three of us remain, stubborn or fearful or – I don't know what keeps Twenty-Six. He never speaks. I dine alone in the garden this morning.

The orb that is not my grandmother gathers my dishes and asks, 'Would you like to begin your departure treatments today?'

'No, but...but I will take a tour.'

The orb pulses with a warm orange glow. 'I will make the arrangements.'

A compact vehicle with three wheels and a comfortably cushioned seat takes me from the facility's courtyard. It speaks to me with an unknown voice, melodious and fluting. My heart stutters at the view as we emerge into the outside world.

Great towers of entwined glass and greenery soar in the distance. The road ahead is more like a wide clearing than the streets I remember. Plants line both sides and grow into structures that sprout from the ground.

'Are these buildings?' I ask.

'They are private dwellings,' my vehicle replies. 'The structures you see farther away are data clusters and production facilities.'

A handful of non-human shapes move along the avenue. After seeing the variety of my caregivers, their eclectic forms don't startle me.

'Why aren't those...people...using vehicles like you?'

'I'm a special purpose volunteer. They can reconfigure if they need to travel faster.'

I sense a note of amusement underlying the words.

My transport moves at a comfortable pace, slow enough that the lack of windows isn't bothersome.

'They're all networked together, right? That's why they aren't talking?'

'Correct, but networked communications are considered a form of speech.'

Birdsong and the rustling of leaves relieve the silence. A blue sky forms a bowl above. Clouds drift across in elongated shapes. The familiar clashes with the strange, and I grip the seat against a sense of vertigo.

'It's rather beautiful,' I whisper. I can't help it.

My artist's eye traces the organic shapes of the landscape and the people. Do they have paint in this time? Canvases? Paper?

A figure appears at an intersection. At first glance, it looks like a human being, and I almost call out a greeting. Then it turns. The eyes are solid silver. It blinks and nods a silent greeting at me, but I am too busy swallowing a gasp to respond.

When I regain my composure, I say, 'Take me back, please.'

———

I come out of sleep feeling disoriented. My room is dark. A hand shakes my shoulder, and I turn on the ceiling light. Anika sits on the floor next to my cot. Her gaunt frame shivers in the chill air and dried tears mark her cheeks.

'I can't sleep. I keep wondering if I'm being a coward. If I'm being ungrateful. What sacrifices did my family make to give me this chance? And I'm going to throw it all away... Not that they're here to care about it.'

I gather my thoughts. 'I took the tour.'

'I know.'

'Here, lie down,' I say and scoot over against the wall to make room.

Her blue eyes widen.

'I don't mean it like that, but you're cold, and I don't mind the company. Please?'

Anika lies next to me, careful to avoid touch, but her body's warmth crosses the gap. I turn out the light. Honesty comes easier in the dark.

'Will you take the treatment tomorrow?' she asks.

'What I saw outside... I'm still scared, but it wasn't all bad. The world they've built is strange, beautiful in its own way.' I find her hand with mine and grasp it gently. 'Maybe – if you want – we can face it together?'

'Do you think they'll let us?'

'There were others who went outside with each other, remember?'

Anika's body relaxes into mine. 'The choice to live – I never thought I'd have to make it.'

I sigh and yawn as my eyelids fall closed. 'Me neither.'

———

'Good morning,' my friend's voice says.

Anika lies in the bed across the room. Sunlight filters through the ceiling of our home. It accents her smiling expression with pale greens. Her skin glitters with a metallic tone, but her eyes are still blue and human-looking, and her braid remains grey. In private, we speak with our natural vocal cords.

They placed us near the sea in an area that used to be Northwestern France. The air reminds me of San Francisco, salt-tinged and fog-laden.

We take our breakfast outside. The Château de Brest sits to our left, across the river, a concession to historical preservation.

'I'd like to paint that,' I say.

'I suspected as much from the way you stare at it,' Anika says. 'I've been researching the chemistry. We can formulate oil and acrylic paints to match what you're used to.'

'After work today?'

'It's a date.'

Our friendship develops new details each day. I know so little about her compared to my old relationships.

I scan the list of day-labour that I qualify for. With my minimal capabilities, my options are few. I choose neighbourhood maintenance. It's the modern equivalent of gardening. To my surprise, Anika's name appears next to mine. Since we began our second life, she's chosen to stay indoors for work.

'I think I'm ready,' she says, anticipating my question.

We bury our dishes in the decomposer and wash up. At the door, Anika hesitates so I take her hand in mine. She nods. I take a deep breath. We step outside together, into our new world.

RUNTIME

The wall behind Marmeg thrummed with the muffled impact of bass beats. A line of girls in heels mixed with boys in lacy shirts, both interspersed with androgynous moots wearing whatever they wanted. Blue light spilled from the club's doorway on to cuffs and bracelets but mostly on bare skin.

The host was a moot with minimal curves of breast and hip, draped in a sheath of satin grey. Candy-coloured red hair in two long curls framed zir face. This host wanted to be seen, and Marmeg had a hard time not looking.

Her own body tended toward her mother's build – no hiding the mammary glands and rounded buttocks. She mitigated it with the torso shell and a neutral haircut while dreaming of moot surgery.

Marmeg glanced at her cuff. Another twenty minutes until the end of her shift. The line drifted forward and two new people came into view. A nat male with waves of silky brown hair and a translucent suit stood near Marmeg, his gaze fixed on the screen in his hands.

'Unbelievable,' he crowed. 'Last round. Canter's winning!'

His friend was a moot with a rainbow 'hawk and a bored expression.

'Fights? Last century much?' Zir red lips curled.

'Races be where's at.'

Zir friend looked up from his screen. 'Minerva starts tomorrow.'

Marmeg's heart pounded. The Minerva Sierra Challenge would be the first race of her life. She was a long shot with her outdated, refurbished embed gear, but one dark horse usually made it to the top five. She planned to be this year's surprise element.

'Be following that, sure,' said Rainbow Hair. 'Minerva's winner trumps the BP International.'

'Not always. Two years ago, remember that? Topsy-turvy all over,' the friend countered.

Their voices faded as the host let them in. Marmeg checked her cuff – fifteen more minutes – and shifted her weight. The host shot her a dirty look. Be invisible: that was Marmeg's role. Here at the club or out in the world, nobody wanted to see the likes of her, but she would be worth noticing soon.

The second-shift bouncers came out on time. Marmeg walked to the bus stop in full gear, drawing surprised glances from the small crowd waiting at the signpost. A faint star forced its light past the competing glow of Los Angeles. Tomorrow night, she would be out in the middle of nothing and nowhere, and then she'd see more than one twinkle. *Star light, star bright, first and only star I see in this concrete clusterf–* The bus arrived.

She climbed in last and sat on a hard plastic chair. The screen above her displayed a white-haired Congressman next to a blonde talk-show host. Their voices blared through tinny speakers.

'US citizenship is a birthright. Voting is a birthright,' the Congressman said. 'But social services – public education, health care, retirement benefits – those need to be earned. Unlicensed families haven't paid into the system.'

The blonde nodded. 'Do you think we should repeal the Postnatal License Act?'

'The problem with postnatal licensing is the barrier to entry: it's too low. The unlicensed pay a small fee – that doesn't scale with age – and then they're like us.'

'Bull,' Marmeg muttered. She'd spent three years saving for her 'small fee'.

Her cuff zapped the skin on the inside of her wrist. She flicked it. The screen lit up and displayed a message from Jeffy.

SORRY TO BUG. SHIT'S GOING DOWN. HELP?

So much for getting a few hours of rest before catching the midnight bus to Fresno. Her brother needed rescuing more often than Marmeg cared to tally, especially right after a club shift. She hopped off the bus at the next stop and used Jeffy's cuff GPS to locate him: Long Beach.

She took the train to the station closest to her brother's location. From there, she ran in long, loping strides. Leg muscles encased by exoskeletons flexed and relaxed in a stronger, more graceful counterpoint than she could have achieved naturally. As she moved, she downloaded new code into the chips controlling her gear. She had developed the software to bypass the legal limits for her embeds. When it came to Jeffy's 'friends', legal wasn't always good enough.

The fight house was a narrow single-storey with a sagging wood porch that had been white at some point. Puddles of stale beer and vomit soaked into the weedy lawn. A cheerful roar rose from the backyard.

Marmeg ran along the right side of the house. A ring of people – mostly nats – blocked her view of the action. She crouched and sprang on to the roof, landing on all fours.

Jeffy reeled in the centre of the crowd. Blood dripped from his nose and left ear. His black curls were plastered to his head by dripping sweat, one hank covering part of a swollen eye. His left leg had an obvious limp. Cords of muscle rippled under his torn shirt. Chestnut skin peeked through the hole.

Her brother hadn't done much after leaving the army, but he maintained a soldier's body. Not that it did him much good in these fights. His lithe opponent, clad in deteriorating exos, kicked him hard in the bad leg. It flew out from under him. He collapsed and lay unmoving.

The crowd cheered. Some of them waved bottles in the air. Others held old-fashioned paper money in their raised fists. Marmeg jumped into the clear centre. The crowd roared again, probably expecting her to fight. Instead, she scooped up her unconscious brother, slung him over her shoulder, and leapt over the crowd. A disappointed groan rose from the onlookers. Marmeg barely heard it. She stumbled on her landing, Jeffy's bulk complicating her balance. She kept to a simple jog on the way to the bus station.

She paid for their bus fare with a swipe of her cuff. The

orange-coloured account balance glared from the screen. The extra cost to rescue her brother was unexpected, but she had enough money to buy her ticket to Fresno, barely.

'Can walk,' Jeffy slurred when they were a few blocks from home.

Fine, let him arrive on his own two feet. He wouldn't be fooling anybody. Marmeg's cuff said it was slightly past ten o'clock, so the boys would be sleeping. That was a small mercy.

They walked in with Jeffy leaning heavily on her shoulder. She hardly felt his weight, but their mother's gaze landed like a sack of stones.

'Again?' Amihan Guinto looked worn out and disappointed as only a parent could. She grunted and stood up from the concave sofa. 'Put him here. I'll take a look.'

'How was your shift?' Marmeg asked as she helped Jeffy lie down. The metal frame creaked under his bulk.

'Miss Stevens missed the bedpan again so I guess it was a normal day,' Amihan said. She rummaged through a kitchen cabinet. 'Take that unnatural junk off, Mary Margaret.'

Marmeg was tempted to refuse, but she needed to do a once-over on her gear anyway. She dropped the parts in a heap. Amihan walked by, carrying the odour of warmed-up chicken adobo and rice with her. Marmeg hadn't eaten since the afternoon, before her shift at the club. Her stomach rumbled as she helped herself to some leftovers while her mother patched up Jeffy's wounds.

Amihan hadn't objected when Marmeg learned to program. She'd expressed cautious optimism when Marmeg began winning contest money, but she had never approved of embeds or moots or any modern trend. *Elective surgery goes against God and the Pope*. Marmeg had heard the words often enough that they were tattooed on her brain.

Her mother had kicked her out after her first chip implant, but Marmeg could easily match her mother for stubbornness. She'd lived on the streets, spending the nights in homeless shelters when she couldn't crash with her friend T'shawn. Luck had landed her some workable exoskeleton discards and then the club security job. The money was enough to split rent with her mother, which let Amihan relent while saving face.

Marmeg washed her plate and then sat with her equipment. Her embedded control chips were legit, but the surgery to put them in wasn't, and her exoskeletal gear was filched from trash bins in rich neighbourhoods. The pieces tended to break. She had backup parts to rube a fix during the race, but she'd rather catch a loose bolt or hairline crack now than in the mountains.

'Have you registered for the certificate programme yet?' Amihan asked.

'Yes,' Marmeg replied, staying focused on the pieces of gear scattered about. She'd filed the forms, not the payment.

'Did you get a spot in the elder care programme?'

'Mm-hmm.'

She had requested a spot, but was stalling the registrar at UCLA with promises of tuition. As long as she placed in the top five in tomorrow's race, she'd have the money to start a four-year embed degree programme. Real degrees led to real money, and that's what she needed to live on her terms, not her mother's.

'I know you're disappointed, mahal, but four-year colleges

won't qualify a postnatal for financial aid. Working in the nursing home isn't that bad.'

'No? Our life is so good?'

'There's food on the table,' Amihan said sharply. 'My children are healthy, except for this idiot.' She nudged Jeffy.

'And all of us born unlicensed.'

'So, we don't get free education and health care. You can't have everything handed to you on a gold plate. Let's be grateful for what God has given us.'

'I am, Ma, but I want more. Six-digit ratings. Big money and benefits jobs. Make some rules, even with no vote. Run the world. Not be run down by it.'

'Are you calling me run-down?'

Marmeg pressed her lips together. She had no safe answer to that question.

'Look at me! Four kids, and my body still looks great. My tits aren't saggy. My ass is nice. When I'm out after my shift, men buy me drinks.'

'That explains the four kids,' Marmeg muttered.

A slap against the back of her head knocked the multi-tool out of her hand.

'Hey! That's –'

'Don't disrespect your mother. My body only bears children when God wants, and I've been married every time.'

'So, He doesn't give a shit if your kids are unhealthy, uneducated, under –'

This time, the blow landed hard across Marmeg's cheek, making her face burn and her eyes sting.

'Take that vile metal filth and get out! Go back to your

club! Surround yourself with those people who deny God's gifts. Go! Ugly, ungrateful child.'

Marmeg clamped down on the surge of answering violence. Even without the exoskeletal enhancements, her body was bigger and stronger than her mother's.

Self-defence or not, if she hurt Amihan, she'd be the one feeling lower than a worm.

'Ma?' said a sleepy voice from the hallway. Then, 'Marmeg!'

A small body clad in faded cupcake pyjamas hurtled into Marmeg. She wrapped her little brother in her arms and glared over his shoulder at their mother. *Your yelling woke them up!*

'It's late, Felix. Go back to bed,' Marmeg said.

The six-year-old was wide awake now, and he spotted Jeffy on the sofa.

'Again?' He almost sounded like their mother.

'He'll be fine,' Marmeg and Amihan said simultaneously.

'Go to sleep, Felix, or you'll be feeling it on your backside.'

Marmeg kissed the soft brown cheek and then stood, picking up her little brother in a smooth motion. 'I'll tuck you in.'

Lee was fast asleep on the upper bunk as Marmeg laid the baby of the family in the lower.

'Tell me a story?' Felix wheedled.

'Not tonight. It's late.'

'You say that every time,' he grumbled.

He had a point. Marmeg left anyway, knowing that Felix would draw her further into the argument if she stuck around. She glanced balefully at their mother. *That was your fault,* she wanted to say, but she kept the peace for the sake of her brothers.

'I'm tired,' Amihan said, some of the shrillness gone from her voice. She walked toward the bedroom. 'I'm going to bed too.'

'Fine,' Marmeg said.

She finished tuning up the exos and then pulled a large nylon backpack from the hall closet. She loaded it with spare parts and repair tools. A shabby plastic poncho went in too, in case the slight chance of rain materialized. The bag was old, with multiple patches of duct tape, but it held. She was about to put it on when Jeffy groaned from the sofa.

'Marm,' he said, motioning her over.

She walked back and knelt by the sofa.

'You goin'? Tonight?'

'Yeah. Midnight bus to Fresno. Six o'clock to Oakhurst. Run or hitch from there. You be okay to watch the littles tomorrow?'

'Don't worry 'bout me. You focus on this race. You got 'nough money?'

As if her brother had any to spare. 'Be okay, long as I place.'

'An' if you don't?'

'But I will.'

'That's my girl. You take care. An' kick some ass, eh?'

Marmeg smiled lopsidedly. 'Hooah.'

She tried to find a clean inch on her brother's face to kiss and settled for the top of his head. He was snoring by the time she reached the front door. A glance at her cuff told her that she couldn't catch the bus in time on foot.

She sent T'shawn a message: NEED A RIDE FROM HOME TO BUS CENTRAL. YOU FREE?

The response came a minute later. BE RIGHT THERE.

Ten minutes later, T'shawn pulled up in an old two-seater that he'd inherited from his uncle. The young man was tall, skinny, and garbed in his typical outfit of baggy jeans and a loose, long-sleeved shirt. His goggles – a relic from age twelve – were wrapped around his head. They were his first project. He'd fit the lenses from his regular glasses into old blue swim goggles that he'd found in the trash near school. When he showed up to classes wearing them, Marmeg was terrified for his safety, but he was so casual and confident that derision fell off him like paint flakes from his car. He did get beaten up later that day, but, as he'd pointed out to Marmeg when she patched him up, the goggles had saved him from yet another pair of broken glasses.

These days, T'shawn had such high black-market ratings that no one with a working brain would harass him. He still wore the goggles.

Marmeg smiled at him as they clasped arms, each one's hand to the other's elbow.

'What got you late?' he said.

The car's electric motor whined to life, and they pulled away from the curb.

'Jeffy had a 404.'

'Gonna get himself killed one day. Can't be rescuing him always, Marm. You almost missed the bus.'

'Know it, but he's my brother. Had my back all these years. Gotta look out.'

T'shawn nodded, then shrugged. 'Be growing up, getting yourself out. You win Sierra, he'll be on his own. Oh, yeah, got some treats for you.'

He took a small case from the car's centre console and handed it to her. Four tiny capsules nestled in grey industrial foam. They gleamed with gold and green.

'New chips?'

T'shawn grinned. His teeth reflected white in the lights of opposing traffic, his face a dark shadow. 'Payback for your latest code. Done my clients real good; said they did parkour times a hundred. Clean getaway last night.'

'Don't tell me.'

'Black market pays.'

'Sure, but don't gotta like it. Want a better way.'

'That's why you racing tomorrow. Don't be grumpy, Marm.'

She smiled. Even if she didn't like his clients, she couldn't hold a grudge against T'shawn. Legit sales channels demanded certifications she couldn't afford. Yet. She closed the case and slipped it into her gear bag. The capsules were identical to the ones Marmeg had in her body. Those had also been rewards from T'shawn and his friends in dark places.

They arrived at the bus station ten minutes before midnight. Marmeg grabbed her bag and stepped out into a cloud of diesel fumes. She coughed and thanked her friend for the ride.

'Good luck,' T'shawn said.

'Owe you for this, brud.'

'It's nada. You go win.'

The car behind them honked. T'shawn rolled his eyes, gave her a salute, and pulled away.

Marmeg walked into the squat concrete bus station. Security guards in bulky exos watched her motions as they did with anyone wearing gear. She found her bus and boarded it. The dozen other passengers were mostly migrant farm workers from Mexico and Southeast Asia. Half of them had already dozed off, and the others were staring at their screens.

Marmeg had a row to herself. Her pack sat next to her, bulky and comforting. She wrapped her arms around it and tried to sleep, to forget the flash of red after she'd paid for the one-way ticket to Oakhurst. Her account was zeroed.

———

The bus from Fresno to Oakhurst arrived late. Marmeg had intended to foot it from the small town to the starting line, but no way would she make it on time. She stood outside the station, staring at the distant peaks in despair. A woman emerged from the building and walked to her.

'I'm headed that way myself,' the woman said. She was obviously middle-aged and a nat, reminiscent of Marmeg's mother. 'Want a lift?'

Thank God for the kindness of strangers.

Marmeg felt the first twinges of motion sickness as the pickup truck bounced and swayed through the curves of Sky Ranch Road. The woman – Lauren was her name – kept her eyes on the uneven dirt road, but she must have sensed Marmeg's discomfort.

'You want to turn back? It's not too late. You can still catch the bus to Fresno.'

Marmeg explained, 'Carsickness, not nerves.' Then she shrugged. 'Can't go back. Account's full busted. Gotta race. Gotta place.'

'How old are you, sweetie? Does your mom or dad know you're up here doing this?'

'Twenty,' Marmeg lied. 'Mom knows.'

They bounced through a particularly vicious dip. Marmeg's head smacked into the truck's ceiling on the rebound.

'Sorry,' Lauren said.

Marmeg stared through the pockmarked but clean windshield. Trees towered above them on both sides. They mostly looked like elongated Christmas trees. Some had rusty red bark with a feathery texture. She was tempted to look them up on her cuff, but the thought of trying to read while her stomach lurched put her off. Every few minutes, she caught a glimpse of rounded granite mounds: the peaks of the Sierra Nevada mountains.

'Here we are,' Lauren said as she turned right into a large dirt clearing.

Dust rose around the truck as they pulled up next to the tree line. Sleek but rugged vehicles were parked nearby. The whole area swarmed with people. Marmeg flicked her wrist to activate her cuff. The time read 8.35. She would not have made the nine o'clock cut-off on foot, not with all the enhancements in the world.

'Thanks,' Marmeg said. 'Owe you big. Credit you some grid time? Call it quits?'

Lauren raised her eyebrows. 'What?'

Marmeg spoke in slower, fuller sentences. 'Can't pay you back for the ride, but I got grid time to spare. Trade for your help. If you want.'

'This was a favour, kid. You don't owe me anything. Just promise me that you'll make it through and back to your mom in one piece, okay? I've got a son not much younger than you. You remind me of him.'

Marmeg ducked her head shyly.

'Deal. You look out tomorrow. See my name.'

Marmeg ignored the bemused look Lauren gave her and hauled her bag out of the back. She waved once as Lauren drove away. Dust stirred in the wake of the tyres, making her sneeze. Its scent reminded her of the housekeeper who lived downstairs and always smelled of pine, though that was harsher than the natural version. Even the air smelled different from home – sharper, simpler.

Marmeg walked across the crowded dirt lot to the race booth. Journos surrounded former winners and high-rated contestants. Marmeg's heart beat faster. She was nobody today, but she knew that a few people had placed bets on her. Her odds were long – this was her first race – but they wouldn't be on her next one, not if she finished Minerva in the top five.

Contestants and their support teams clustered in small groups. Most had their screens out for last-minute tune-ups and optimized settings. A few were warming up. *Flashing their feathers*, Marmeg thought. She felt more than saw their curious glances as she walked by. Somebody snickered. Marmeg was glad of her brown skin. It hid the flush.

The registration booth was a modest structure made of canvas and plastic. A giant electronic panel across its top looked out of place as it displayed vid clips from previous Minerva Challenges. The corporate logo – a clockwork owl – hung on a banner to the left with the words EQUIPPING THE ATHLETES OF THE FUTURE printed below.

Two people sat behind the booth table. The one who faced outward was an attractive moot with short, floppy blond hair and a toothy smile. The other had zir back to Marmeg.

She dropped her gear bag on the dirt and waved her cuff over the screen on the table. It came to life and filled with upside-down text next to her picture.

'Mary Margaret Guinto?' the blond read.

Marmeg nodded.

Zie frowned. 'Where's your support team? They need to check in too.'

'My, uh, team?' Marmeg struggled to recall the race application and requirements. 'They're late. Be here soon.'

The other person behind the table turned around, and Marmeg startled at seeing zir – his – beard. She had assumed everyone here would be a moot.

'They need to meet you on the far side,' he said, also frowning. He bent over the screen and flicked through Marmeg's registration. 'You didn't put their names in the application. We'll need their information and your emergency contact's as well.'

Marmeg scribbled three names with her index finger into the blank fields: Jefferson Marcos, Lee Inciong, Felix Inciong. Her brothers were the first people Marmeg could think of who didn't have a criminal record. Not that it would matter if the Minerva reps bothered to look them up – two of them were underage. She listed Amihan as her emergency contact.

Beard-guy rotated the display to face Marmeg. Tiny, dense text filled the page.

'Fingerprint at the bottom,' he instructed.

Marmeg glanced over the section headers as she scrolled through pages of rules, regulations, waivers, and exclusions. She knew the rules well enough. The rest didn't matter. She pressed her thumb against the sensor. The blond grabbed Marmeg's other wrist, injected a subdermal chip, and slapped a Band-Aid over it.

'Race ID,' zie explained. 'Good luck, and see you on the other side.'

Start time was in an hour. Marmeg found an unoccupied space near the trees to do a final gear check of her own. She examined the pins on the leg ports, making sure their alignment was good and the screws were tight. The torso shell came next. It made her feel like a turtle, but it was the best she had found in the castoff bin behind the used gear shop.

'What is zie wearing? Second generation exos?' said someone nearby.

'I think you mean *she*.'

'Why are you picking on her, Zika?' asked a third, more melodious voice. 'Worried about the competition? She's brave to even go out in that kit.'

Marmeg kept her body relaxed and ignored them. Doing security at the club had given her a fairly thick skin. She pulled muscle-enhancing sleeves over her arms and stuffed the skeletal-looking braces in the bag, hoping she wouldn't need to climb any overhangs. The braces only half-worked on the best of days. A quick systems check on her screen showed everything powered up and responding correctly.

An enormous tree trunk lay fallen at an angle a few yards away. Marmeg walked over to it. Its high point came up to her shoulders. She flexed her legs, crouched, and leapt to the top, landing lightly on the crumbling wood. A few heads turned to stare at her, and she quirked her lips. They wanted a show? Fine. She flipped backward off the tree, sprung off her hands, twisted mid-air, and landed on all fours.

Her audience shook their heads and returned to their tasks. Irked by the lukewarm reaction, Marmeg pulled her screen from the backpack and found the software she'd given T'shawn. *Parkour times a hundred.* She loaded the code into her chips.

She stood and flexed, testing the reaction time and spring coefficients. A mound of granite boulders the size of a small house was her target. She ran toward it. Cool alpine wind brushed her cheeks. Pine needles crackled underfoot. Crouch. Jump. Right foot on a near-vertical wall of rock. Push off. Land on the balls of the feet. Keep the momentum! Up, sideways with a hand and foot, diagonal. Pause.

She stopped for a few seconds at the highest point and chose her next target. She jumped, grabbed a branch, swung, flipped, and landed lightly enough to go straight into a run. Her breath came hard as she arrived at her gear bag. The air was sweet but thin. Marmeg didn't have the luxury of arriving a few nights early to let her body acclimate to the altitude.

'See that, Zika?' said the voice from earlier. 'Maybe Cinderella will make it to the ball.'

Marmeg almost laughed out loud. *My fairy godmother isn't done with her tricks.* She sipped at her water and then pulled up a motion analysis on her screen. A few tweaks to the rebound settings, and next time she'd be able to run up the rock without using her hands.

Her cuff buzzed – two new messages and fifteen minutes to start time. Marmeg repacked her gear bag, cinching everything tight, and slung it over her shoulders as she walked to the trailhead. A cluster of people clad in smartskin and carrying next to nothing already stood there with distant gazes. Their lips moved and fingers twitched.

Someday, Marmeg promised herself, *I'll have all of that.* Maybe even someday soon. She checked her messages.

WHERE ARE YOU? IF YOU'VE RUN AWAY FROM HOME, DON'T BOTHER COMING BACK: that was from her mother.

The second was T'shawn: GIVE ME YOUR GEAR IF YOU TOAST OUT?

OVER MY DEAD BODY, she sent back.

She ran a final download of map and satellite information before deactivating her grid access. That was the primary constraint of the Minerva Challenge. Stale data and live GPS would have to carry her through the race. The second requirement was to traverse a minimum of seventy-five miles before crossing the finish line on the eastern side of the Sierras. The record holder, from two years past, finished at a minute over eighteen hours.

The sun blazed through the heavy clouds for one eye-dazzling second, making Marmeg squint. When she looked around again, the crowd at the staging point had increased. A giant clock counted up to 10:00 am on the screen above the registration booth.

'Double, double, toil and trouble,' Marmeg muttered.

The person next to her, shiny from head to toe, smiled.

'What are you brewing?' zie said.

'Not me. Them.' Marmeg inclined her head at the booth. 'Stirring up some drama.'

'I suppose they are. It's not like seconds or minutes matter at the finish. If they really wanted to make some excitement, they'd be funding Mountain Mike. So, is this your first race?'

'Yes. What's mountain mike?'

'Not what. Who,' zie said, sounding amused. 'He's a radical nat who lives in the backcountry. They always get a glimpse of him around the biggest accident sites, but they can't seem to catch him. You'd think it would be simple, him being a nat and all. Maybe living off-grid makes it easy to disappear.'

Marmeg frowned. She hadn't planned for crazy forest nats.

'Don't look so worried,' zie said with a laugh. 'I think he's mostly a scare story. There are worse things for you to worry about. Like the rain. And have you deactivated your grid access? If it's on at the start, that's an instant disqualification. They're checking, you know?' Zie gestured at the camera drones buzzing overhead. 'Those aren't all journos.'

'It's off,' Marmeg said.

Yes, her cuff showed that grid access was disabled. No more messages. No more support. She was on her own.

The clock display had switched to a countdown timer. Ten seconds to go. Someone called a verbal version through the booth speakers. Drone-cams buzzed. Thunder rumbled in the distance.

'Good luck.'

'You too.'

'Zero!' boomed a voice.

The race opened like sand pushing through the neck of an hourglass. The lead contestants took off down the main trail at an easy run. Marmeg kept herself in their midst. A swarm of cameras flew above them, tracking every move and narrating the action to faraway viewers.

Being in the lead at the start had no correlation to being in the winners' list at the end, but it did boost your ratings. Most viewers only paid attention to the crowd during the open and the finish. The rest of the race belonged to the pros who could record and sell their whole experience as movies.

Marmeg pushed her body and her gear hard. A few heads turned in surprise as she passed them. Her breath came fast and shallow, but she gained until only three people remained ahead of her. If nothing else, she was in the top five at this moment.

They sprinted together over rocks and fallen trees. Dodged the grasping branches of low-growing bushes. Curved around trunks as wide as the pillars of City Hall. A cool wind brought the smell of rain.

The lead cluster spread out over the course of the first thirty minutes. People split off to follow their predetermined routes or took alternate ways around ponds and meadows.

The other runners became blurs flitting between columnar trunks, far enough to be unobtrusive. The last drone camera had turned back at the twenty-minute mark, pushing the limits of its range.

Marmeg leapt on a fallen tree and used it to cross a boggy section. She skirted a car-sized knot of rotten wood at the far end and stopped to get her bearings. The other contestants had disappeared from sight. Like the fingers of a river delta, they would follow unique paths to the finish line. Her own route headed northeast toward the first of many low ridges.

As Marmeg ran, she heard nothing but the whispers of her footfalls and the wind through the trees. The rushing sound reminded her of rice pouring from a burlap sack. *Don't think about food*, she told herself. The clouds grew darker as she gained elevation. The air thinned and cooled. The light was dim for midday. Marmeg stopped to get a kinetic charger out of her gear bag and strap it to her left arm. Her cuff had solar cells, but they wouldn't be of much use in this weather.

She set her pace at a jog, leaping over the occasional fallen tree. Once, she startled a squirrel as she landed on the far side of a trunk. Had it been a snake, she could've been out of the race, like two years back when a contestant needed air rescue for a rattlesnake bite. She avoided blind jumps after that.

Heavy drops of rain spattered Marmeg as the trees dwindled. The pale hue of granite filled the widening gaps between reddish-brown trunks. In minutes, the woods went from sparse to non-existent, replaced by boulders and twiggy bushes. A towering ridge rose from the open ground. Slabs of grey laced with pale blue and white loomed like sloppy icing on her mother's homemade cakes.

Marmeg grinned and raised her wrist to take a picture. Her brothers would be amazed that she'd climbed over this. Raindrops fell faster as she leapt from one mound to the next, the muscles of her legs reacting with unnatural force, driven by the exoskeleton. The journey to the top of the ridge was a dance. Jump. Twist. Take three delicately balanced steps to the left. Jump again.

A cramp in her right calf forced her to stop and adjust the exo's settings. Marmeg breathed heavily and took a break to look around from the high point. She stood on an island of stone surrounded by conical tips of dark green, a sea that undulated and shifted in colour depending on the terrain. In the distance, sheets of rain obscured the serrated peaks that awaited her. Lightning flickered in her periphery.

She stared, unblinking, until she saw one strike in full. The jagged, white-hot flash was a phenomenon she'd never seen in her eighteen years of life in Los Angeles. Alone on the ridge, she thought to herself: *This must be how God felt after creating the world.*

A loud crack from behind brought her back to mortality. Lightning preferred to strike at exposed locations. She would be safer in the forest. Marmeg descended the ridge, favouring speed over grace. When she reached the shelter of trees, she slowed down. Rain trickled down her head in steady rivulets. The precipitation made a gentle rustle as it fell through the alpine canopy. The air had become noticeably cooler, and her wet state wasn't helping. Marmeg activated the heating coils in the torso shell.

Twenty minutes later, her breath came out in cottony white puffs, and she was colder than ever. She slipped a hand under the shell to confirm what she suspected: it hadn't warmed up.

Muttering curses in Tagalog that she'd learned from her mother, she stopped and reached into her pack. Her hand found the soft bundle of spare clothing.

Marmeg slipped out of the torso shell and sleeves. Goosebumps popped up along her bare arms. She pulled on a thermal shirt and a fleece sweatshirt with a faded US Army logo. Back on went the gear, and over that, the dollar-store plastic rain poncho. At least the torso shell's abdominal activators and cardio monitor still worked.

Some semblance of warmth returned after Marmeg jogged for a mile through the sodden trees. Her steps converged to an even rhythm. Her mind wandered to daydreams. She would finish her degree in embed design and get a 'benefits job', as people said back home. If she was lucky, the company would pay for additional enhancements and surgeries. Then, once she was sufficiently buffed, she could quit and become a professional racer.

The pros had embedded audio and video recording capabilities with stereo sensors for immersive playback. The best had haptic sensors for whole-body virtual reality. Not many in the general public could use that level of technology, but the day was coming when they would. She had to become a star before that happened. That was the way out of the nat ghetto, to go from cash to credit to rich on ratings. This race was only the first step.

When she made it as a big-time embed racer, she could get her brothers in on the game. T'shawn, too. They could be her legit support team. Maybe Felix would grow up to become an embed developer too. They could live in an actual house with separate bedrooms, and she would never have to share a bathroom again. Or worry about someone eating her food. She wouldn't even have to think about food, because she would hire someone to keep their fridge well stocked.

Best of all, if she were rich, she could have moot surgery and maybe convince her younger brothers to do the same. Jeffy was a lost cause, though he didn't hate moots like their mother did. And what would Amihan say about Marmeg's success? She would have to take back every nasty, negative comment she'd made about Marmeg's looks or smarts. She might even get licensed grandkids. Marmeg would gladly gift Jeffy the fees if he could stay with one girl long enough.

Her cuff beeped. She was off course by a quarter mile. She stopped running and traced a corrected path. Her sweat cooled. She shivered and looked up at the grey skies. They'd grown darker and more swollen with rain. *Keep moving, stay warm.*

She headed toward a mountain pass, the first of several on her planned route. The pass had looked smooth in the satellite images, an easy way to cross the first range. Maybe she'd meet another contestant there, though she knew the pros would prefer a challenge. Their sponsors paid for drama. This route did not promise excitement.

Marmeg was damp, chill, and borderline miserable when she arrived at the rock pile marking the climb to the pass. The rain had eased to a sprinkle. Cold had settled in its place like a determined, unwelcome houseguest.

Someone stood at the cairn. Marmeg was momentarily relieved at the sight of another human being, but she hung back, out of zir line of sight. Would this person be a friend or a foe? Given her mixed reception at the staging area, zie was as likely to scoff at or even sabotage her as zie was to be helpful. If only she could look up zir ratings on the grid, she would know the answer in seconds.

The person was staring at the space in front of zir face. Looking at maps, Marmeg assumed. She gathered her courage.

'Hoy,' she called, coming forward.

Zie turned and focused on her. Zir eyes were almost black in the gloomy afternoon light. They were framed by long, curving lashes. This one definitely looked moot, with dark brown skin and curly black hair much like Marmeg's, though zie wore it to zir shoulders. It hung damp and limp in ropy waves. Zie had the slightest hint of curves at chest and hip, enough to be alluring but not enough to give away what zie was born with. Zie showed little sign of wetness and no signs of cold, wrapped as zie was in an expensive-looking smartskin.

'Hello. Are you headed up to the pass too?' Zie had an accent that Marmeg couldn't place.

'Firm.'

'Pardon?'

'Yes. Up the pass.'

'Great. We can walk up together if you don't mind the company.'

Zie was rather cute. She wouldn't mind spending an hour with zir, and they'd have plenty of time to split up and get back to racing on the other side. *All or nothing,* she thought.

'Let's go.'

They walked along something that resembled a path but was more of a clearing between scraggly bushes, boulders, and twisted trees. They made a course correction whenever one of them spotted the next stack of rocks that marked the way.

'My name is Ardhanara Jagadisha, but that seems to be a mouthful for Americans. You can call me Ardha.'

'Arda,' Marmeg repeated, trying to shape the unfamiliar sound.

'Close enough,' zie said with a friendly smile. 'So, what brings you to this contest?'

Chatty sort. Not her type after all.

'Prize money,' Marmeg said.

Ardha let a few beats of silence pass. Zie must have been expecting more from her.

'I see. My father works for the Lucknow branch of Minerva, and the division there sponsored me to enter the contest. I'm mostly here to field-test their new technology, but the division wants publicity, too. If I win, they'll be able to push for an expansion of the design centre there. I'm studying electrical engineering. I might even work there someday.'

'Where's Lucknow?' Marmeg said, trying to keep up with zir words and strides. Ardha's smartskin was much lighter than Marmeg's old exoskeleton frames, and zie wasn't carrying a pack.

'India,' Ardha said, sounding surprised. Zie waved at zirself. 'You couldn't tell where I'm from?'

Marmeg shook her head.

'No tells on you. Full moot, full embed, right? It's good.'

Ardha looked pleased.

'My grandparents are very progressive. They funded the sex surgery. For the embeds, I only had to pay for the implants. My sponsors donated the rest. So far, everything is holding up quite nicely. And your gear? Where is it from?'

Marmeg flushed as she thought about what to say. The truth wouldn't matter now, out here with no grid access and no way to update their ratings.

'Gear's filched, mostly,' she confessed. 'Got some legit chips – arms, legs, body.' She tapped the base of her skull for the last one.

'What's "filched"? I'm not familiar with that term.'

'From a Dumpster. What some loaded embed threw out.'

'So, you picked up your gear from...a garbage bin?' Ardha's face wrinkled in repulsion and then smoothed into neutrality. 'We're very careful to recycle all of our used gear so that it doesn't fall into criminal hands. Of course, there's so much corruption back home that the real criminals are running the country. That's a different problem. So, isn't this filched gear broken?'

'Fix it. Rube it.' Marmeg shrugged. 'Been doin' since I was eight.'

Ardha's eyebrows shot up. 'You've been repairing embed

gear since you were eight years old? You must be very bright. How many sponsors do you have?'

'Nada.'

Ardha turned and stared at Marmeg.

'Zero,' she clarified.

'Yes, I understood that. I was simply speechless. Unusual for me, I know,' zie said. 'But how is this possible?'

'Born unlicensed. Bought my own later, but sponsors don't like that. Amnesty parents, kids – too much control. Can't use us to sell their stuff.'

'Ah, yes. I had forgotten about the new American caste system. If you're racing without any sponsorship, what will you do if you can't finish? There's a heavy fine for being extracted mid-race. You know that?'

Marmeg shrugged again.

Something small and white drifted by. Then another. And another.

'Snow?'

'So it seems. I didn't see that in the weather forecast. Did you?'

Marmeg shook her head.

'This should make the race more interesting.'

Ardha reached back and pulled up a snug-fitting hood around zir head. Only zir face was exposed now. Tiny white flakes landed on zir brows and eyelashes, glittering there for a few seconds before melting away. Zir breath came in gentle puffs.

Marmeg, working much harder, exhaled clouds of white. She wished she had thought to pack a warm hat. It hadn't occurred to her that they would need winter weather gear in late spring, especially in California.

The snow smelled incredible, somewhere between iced vodka and fresh rain. Bare mountain rock surrounded them. They'd left the trees behind and below. Up here, the only colours were wet cement, gunmetal greys, and white. The clouds hung heavy and close. Wind batted down at them and tossed tiny snowflakes into demented, gravity-defying spirals.

Marmeg squinted, trying to see how much farther they had, but the slope and weather combined to make that a challenge. Ardha saw what she was doing and did the same.

'Oh, bloody hell,' zie said.

'What?'

'You'll see in a minute. Come on.'

Ardha must have enhanced zir distance vision. Zie broke into a run as the granite surface flattened into a gentle incline. Marmeg followed. They stopped abruptly just before the ground turned white. A field of ice stretched before them, all the way up to the top of the pass. Sheer vertical walls of stone rose up on either side. All Marmeg could see through the gap was sky.

'Can you believe it? A glacier! I studied the satellite images extensively. This pass was supposed to be completely clear.' Zie kicked at the ice. 'We'll have to go back and take a different route.'

'Nah. Let's rube it,' Marmeg said.

She sat and pulled out every metal item from her bag, spreading them on the ground until it looked like she was surrounded by shrapnel. Ardha stared as if she had lost her mind. Marmeg ignored zir and examined one item after another. Most were spare parts for her leg and arm exos – screws, pistons, actuators. The screws were too small, but the multi-tool with screwdrivers and blades? That had potential.

Marmeg showed Ardha the small device. 'Cut this up. Strap on the sharp bits. Could get us over.'

'Are you serious?'

'Yeah.'

'You'd help me through the pass?'

'Sure. Splitsville after.'

'That's...very sportsmanlike of you.'

'Got a prob, though.' Marmeg looked at the rest of the debris. 'No metal cutters.'

Ardha held out zir left hand as if zie wanted to shake. A sharp, two-inch-long blade pushed out of zir palm, just below zir pinky finger. Blood welled around the base of the blade, then congealed quickly into a brown scab.

'It will cut through metal like butter, or so they promised me. I didn't think I'd need it, but one of the engineers insisted. Give me the army knife.'

Marmeg placed the multi-tool into Ardha's right hand and tried not to look envious. As the engineers had predicted, Ardha's blade sheared the hinge off with no effort. The various tools slid out and fell to the ground.

'Got a drill, too?'

'Yes. Right here in my index finger.'

Ardha retracted the blade, and Marmeg watched in fascination as zir skin speed-healed over the wound. A small drill bit poked through zir right index finger. Marmeg pulled off her boots.

'Drill here and here,' she said, pointing.

The drill made the barest whine as Ardha punctured the reinforced carbon steel lining of her boots. Ardha's boots were much thinner, and zie put holes in them to match hers. While zie worked on zir boots, Marmeg attached the tools – one screwdriver tip and one short blade for each foot. It was a poor substitute for crampons, but their enhanced balance could make up for it.

'The pass must have been in shadow for the latest satellite images,' Ardha grumbled as zie worked. 'I don't see how else we could have missed the ice. Do you?'

Marmeg nodded. 'Sure. Image hack. Get a high-rater to post it. Fooled us, yeah?'

Ardha frowned. 'I hadn't thought of that.'

Marmeg pulled on her boots. Her toes were stiff with cold, and she wiggled them against the interior to get back some warmth.

'I should have asked them to include a routine for walking on ice. If only we were allowed grid access, I could download one.'

'Could code one.'

'Here? Now? Write an ice-walking routine?'

Marmeg had her screen out and was scanning the subroutine that handled slip and balance. 'Needs a few adjustments. Tweak the numbers in here. Might help.' She blew on her fingers to warm them up and typed in an option to run with lower friction. If it didn't work, she'd need a quick way to return to her normal settings.

'Can I use your software?'

'What chips you got?'

Ardha didn't carry a screen – zie didn't need one – so Marmeg waited for zir to read her the information. The verdict was a no. Ardha's chips were a new design with a new instruction set. She didn't carry compilers for it.

'Sorry,' she said, downloading the new routines into her legs. 'You got a compiler?'

Zie shook zir head. 'I don't even have source code. It was worth a try, though. I can't believe you can write code on the spot like this.'

'Did contests in school. Gotta work fast.'

Marmeg was happy to have come this far without having to fix any equipment. Her cuff showed three hours and eleven miles, well below the record-setting pace, but she wasn't after a record. Even fifth place awarded enough cash to buy one semester's tuition and Felix's license.

'Are you ready?' Ardha said, standing gracefully on zir cobbled boots and holding out a hand.

Marmeg quirked an eyebrow and pointedly ignored zir as she pulled on her pack. She crawled over to the ice field and cautiously stood. She slipped a bit with the first few steps. Then her gyros, chips, and brain figured out how to dance on ice.

Ardha was now holding out both zir arms as if to catch her. It reminded her of a live ballet performance she'd seen years ago with her mother.

'Wanna dance?' she said with a wide grin.

Ardha laughed. 'I'd rather race.' Zie took off up the snowbound slope with rapid but choppy steps.

'Cheat!' Marmeg called after zir.

Then she tried leaping, inspired by the thought of ballerinas. She reached down mid-jump to one leg, then the other, increasing the spring tension. In less than a minute, she leapt past Ardha. The software routine worked beautifully.

Exhilaration soared when she arrived at the top. A glance back showed Ardha jumping but also slipping and counterbalancing as zir smartskin failed to accommodate for rubed crampons. Zir face was drawn with concentration, eyes scanning the ice for the best course.

From the peak of the pass, Marmeg caught her first view of the vastness ahead. Waves upon waves of sharp, rocky peaks continued out to the horizon. Many were shrouded in clouds, and the valley itself was obscured by the haze of falling snow and rain. Somewhere, on the far side of it all, lay the striated columns of Devils Postpile and the finish line.

Ardha stopped next to her, admiration clear on zir face. 'Thank you for the assistance. That saved me at least thirty minutes of rerouting.' Zie reached down and snapped off the blades from zir boots.

'Keep them.'

'I would, but I have no pockets.'

They both laughed. It was true: zir smartskin was smooth and almost featureless. Marmeg took the blades back, snapped off her own, and stowed them in her pack.

When she straightened, Ardha wrapped her in a brief but

gentle hug. Her friend – because it seemed that's what they were now – had a warm, smooth cheek that smelled subtly of roses.

'See you on the other side. Good luck!'

'Luck,' Marmeg replied.

The embrace had startled her, but she didn't mind it. As Ardha pulled away, Marmeg caught a flicker of motion in the corner of her eye.

'Did you see –' she said, but zie was already running down the slope.

Marmeg looked around but didn't see any signs of life. Odd, she thought. Perhaps an animal, though anything big that was up this high was not something she wanted a good look at. She recalled the story about Mountain Mike. A tingle of fear ran through her. Then a sudden gust of wind almost knocked her over and loosed the feeling from her head.

There was no one there but her, and she had to move. Marmeg flicked her wrist and pulled up the route map on her cuff. It headed in a different direction from the way Ardha had run. Zir silver form shrank in the distance. *Good.* She didn't want to spend too much time getting friendly with the competition.

———

The weather worsened as Marmeg traversed the undulating wilderness. Down she went into the quiet of trees, green and gloom, damp earth and soggy pine needles. Up, through scrub and rock, over a small rise with a local view. Down again. Her

steps treacherous as ice crystallized in the shade. She climbed
and descended until the repetition became mind-numbing.

Three hours and thirteen miles passed by with no company
but an occasional squirrel dashing for shelter. Once in a while,
Marmeg heard a rustling sound – usually when she'd stopped
to catch her breath or tweak her leg settings – but she never
spotted the source of the noise. Deer? Bear? She didn't have
any weapon but the broken multi-tool blades, and those would
offer poor protection against an angry or hungry animal. Better
that the creature stayed hidden.

She was leaping cautiously up a rock-strewn ridge, now
speckled with patches of invisible ice, when her right arm froze
in mid-swing. That threw off her already delicate balance. She
came crashing down into a nearby bush.

Marmeg winced as she tried to stand. Her left hip was
bruised, and her arm was locked into a right angle. She got
up awkwardly and walked to a sheltered rock under a tree.
Using her working arm, she tried to pull off the right sleeve.
It was completely rigid. She took her screen out of the pack,
unrolled it, and pulled up the diagnostic software.

A quick check of the sleeve showed everything reading
normal. With a grimace of annoyance, Marmeg called up its
controller chip next. Every register read back an ominous set
of zeroes. She tried sending the reset code, but it made no
difference. Either the chip or its communications was fried.

Marmeg looked up into the feathery dark-green needles
and let out a stream of curse words that she'd learned from one
of her stepfathers. Now what? She could try to keep running
with a locked arm. She could cut the damn sleeve off, though

it would be worthless forever after. Or she could give up, turn on her grid access, and quit.

The third option wasn't a real choice. Not yet, though the likelihood of her placing in the top five was looking a lot lower than it had ten minutes before. Fixing the sleeve would take too much time, but she might as well preserve it as long as possible.

Her hip throbbed, probably from landing on a rock. Her right shoulder ached from the weight of the frozen arm. She chose the first option.

Marmeg grabbed the stim pills out of the backpack and downed two. Then she pulled out an old leg sleeve that she'd brought as backup gear and used it to make a sling. She shivered as she stood. The cold had seeped in quickly while she sat still. She headed onward in a slow jog, wary of every obstacle.

———

An hour later, the weather went from bad to worse as rain turned to sleet and intermittent hail. Marmeg's plastic hood grew heavy with ice crystals. Her leg motions became sluggish. The temperature must have dropped low enough to thicken the hydraulic fluid.

She was halfway across a fallen tree over a raging stream when the leg exos stopped working. Marmeg was stuck like a horse rider in a glitched fantasy game, both legs completely immobile. She tried to warm up the pistons with her mobile hand, but that had no effect.

No way could she remove her exoskeletons while perched ten feet above frigid, frothing water. Instead she scooted, a painstaking few inches at a time, until she was on the other side. There, she swung one leg over the top and landed on her knees in a soggy clump of ferns.

'Are you testing me?' Marmeg said out loud.

Her mother's God might or might not have been listening, but she was tired of being alone. And just plain tired. The cuff showed the time as five-thirty and her mileage at twenty-nine – less than four miles per hour and well under the four-point-two record, but not bad, either. Where was everyone else, she wondered, and how were they faring in this weather?

The background image on her cuff switched to a picture of her brothers. Seeing their faces made tears sting the backs of her eyes.

'Want to go home,' she whispered to the cuff.

Off-grid as she was, nobody would be listening.

'I'm cold. One of my chips is fried. Ice is falling from the sky. Forecast said rain. This isn't rain! Okay, God? You got that? Want me to fail? Teaching me a lesson, like Ma always said you would? Well, screw you! I'm not a quitter.'

The words were a small comfort against the constant patter and crunch of frozen droplets making their way through the trees. Marmeg repeated the last few words like a chant while unscrewing and removing the leg braces. After they were off, it occurred to her to check the embedded chips in her legs.

All four were toast.

Marmeg's scream ripped through the silence and faded into the gentle chatter of precipitation. She kicked viciously at one of the exos. It flew into the muddy, half-frozen stream bank. Her mind reeled. How could five of her embedded chips choose this day, this race, to stop working?

Virus, whispered a voice in the back of her brain.

The chips had programmable boot codes, ones that Marmeg could access using the near-field emitter from her screen. The last time she'd been up close with other people was back at the race start. Someone must have planted the virus with a built-in delay, like a ticking time bomb.

She tested the core chip, the one lodged in her brain stem, and almost cried with relief when it responded correctly. She wiped its memory and reloaded clean code from her screen. That one, at least, wouldn't fall victim to the virus. She did the same for her left arm.

What next? The sun wouldn't set for three hours, but it was getting close to the mountain peaks in the west. The sky was dark with clouds, and the air wasn't getting any warmer. She was facing down a long, cold night with ordinary legs, no heat, and no shelter.

Bail out, she thought. *It's over. You can't win this. You'll be lucky not to freeze to death.*

Then she remembered the spare chips, the last-minute gift from T'shawn, that she'd tucked into her gear bag.

'Crazy talk,' Marmeg whispered.

But her left hand moved, took the small blade from the broken-up multi-tool, sliced through the right sleeve. She wouldn't attempt surgery with only one arm. With both arms free and mobile, she rummaged inside the pack until she found the box.

Four clear capsules nestled in dark grey foam. Inside them, tiny wafers of silicon and gold gleamed in the half-light of late afternoon. Delicate threads of wire lay coiled beside each capsule, the ends surrounded by a protective sheath.

Marmeg had been awake for the original surgeries. T'shawn had held her hand. They'd watched in fascination as Marmeg's leg was numbed; as the surgeon sliced into the flesh of her calf; as he pulled up a quarter-inch flap of bloody skin and muscle. Then he'd tucked a capsule into the incision, threading the lead wires into the muscle fibres, and stitched it up neatly.

Marmeg rolled up one pant leg and traced the old scar with an icy finger. The stim pills ran through her veins, but they wouldn't help much with this. She gritted her teeth, took a deep breath, and pushed the short, dull knife into the scar.

An agonized groan turned into a sob. Blood welled and fell on to the spring green leaves of the fern below like crimson rain. With a trembling hand, Marmeg reached into the cut. She whimpered as she felt for the capsule. When she touched something hard and slippery, she grabbed and yanked. The leads pulled free of the muscle. Adrenaline and endorphins surged. Her heart raced.

The sudden wrench of her stomach caught Marmeg by surprise. She bent over to the side and managed not to throw up on herself. Then, taking a few shaky breaths, she carefully removed a new capsule, unwound the leads, and pushed it into her leg. She shoved the leads apart as best as she could, and then stopped. There was nothing to suture with, not that she even knew how.

Frustration and despair took over like fog filling a valley. Her heart hammered. *Think, you stupid, lousy brain! You wanted to do this race. You thought you could take these people, but you're useless! Just another crapshoot filcher who doesn't know a damn thing about being an embed.*

Glue.

She had glue in the pack.

Marmeg found the small tube of industrial-strength fixative. *Don't glue your fingers to your leg.* She sobbed and laughed. She stanched as much blood as she could with the ruined sleeve and then squeezed glue along the outer part of the incision. She pressed down with one hand while wrapping the useless, ripped fabric around her leg like a bandage. With a shaky sigh of disbelief, she sat back and stared at her handiwork.

'Not bad, but what'll you use to tie off the other three?' a deep voice said from behind.

Marmeg screamed, leapt up, and then cried out from the pain in her calf. In the shadows of the trees stood a tall, wiry man with a face from a nightmare: dark, dirt-streaked skin, wild hair to his shoulders, features hidden behind a coarse beard. Marmeg's tiny blade was lying on the ground. It might as well have been on the moon.

'What – who are you?'

'Let's save the introductions for later. Right now, we need to get you warm and clean that wound up before you contract a raging infection.'

The words took a minute to penetrate the fear pounding through her head.

'Why?'

He raised a bristly eyebrow. 'Why what?'

'Why help me?'

'Don't trust me, eh? Well, that's not a bad instinct for a kid like you in a place like this. Too bad you didn't think of it earlier when you were with the other racer. Now come on. Save your questions for when we're inside. I swear I'm not going to hurt you.'

The man grabbed Marmeg's muddy exos and the rest of her gear, including the bloodied blade, and shoved it all into her pack. He pulled the bag on to his back with a grunt.

'What the hell is in here? Weighs as much as a small person.'

'Gear.'

He snorted, then tried to put an arm around Marmeg. She instinctively twisted away and shoved, but she was the one who lost her balance and fell on the ground. He looked at her with a bemused expression.

'Fine. You go ahead and walk on your own.'

He moved away, threading a path between the plants and trees. Marmeg limped after him.

———

A short but painful walk brought them to a log cabin. The low building nestled under the trees next to a lush, green meadow. The mountain man pushed open a wooden door. Marmeg followed him into a one-room cabin. A cot, a table, and a tree stump stool made up the furnishings. A locked metal chest was tucked under the table. Across from the door, in the corner, stood an oblong black thing, about the size of a large pot, with a metal tube leading out of it and through the roof. Dim light filtered in through a dirty window.

The man busied himself with the black device, pushing small pieces of wood in through a door in its front. Then he grabbed a box, took out a toothpick-looking thing, and struck it against the side. The toothpick lit up, and he tossed it in with the wood. As Marmeg watched in fascination, the smaller pieces caught fire, and soon everything started to burn.

The man noticed her fixed gaze. 'It's a wood-burning stove.'

'Not legit.'

'That's true. It's illegal in California to burn anything that smokes, but it's the only way to survive out here.'

'You Mountain Mike?'

His eyes twinkled. 'Is that what they're calling us?'

Marmeg caught the plural. 'Who else?'

'We're a network. Now, enough standing around. You'd better lie on the bed while I look at that hack job you did on your leg.'

The stove warmed the cabin. Marmeg sank on to the cot, wary but glad of the comfort. The mattress had lumps and smelled mouldy, but it was better than a bed of pine needles. Pain wrenched at her leg as she swung it on to the pallet.

Mike, or whoever he was, had removed a plastic box with basic medical supplies from the metal trunk. He placed the stool next to the bed, sat, and cut away her makeshift bandage. His face twisted into a grimace as he examined the wound.

'I can't do much, but I'll disinfect the outside and cover it with sterile gauze. You'll have to get it looked at tomorrow after you're back in civilization. What I can do,' he said, glancing briefly at her before looking back at the leg, 'is help you with the other calf chip. I've got rubbing alcohol to clean off that knife blade some, and I can make a better incision than you can. Will you let me?'

Marmeg winced as he applied the ointment. If he'd wanted to hurt her or kill her, he could've done so by now, and she could use the help. Then again, nothing in life was free.

'Why? What you want of me?'

'Your word that when you win this race, you'll help our movement.'

'Help how?'

'You give us half your prize money.'

'Half! If I don't?'

'We'll provide evidence to Minerva of this encounter – that you took help from me – and they'll disqualify you and take their money back.'

'If I don't place?'

'You will. You might even come in first. The people we help always end up in the top three.'

Marmeg frowned. 'All cheats? Every year?'

'The last four years. That's when we first got the idea. I suppose it's cheating, but it's a win-win situation the way I see it. We choose someone who deserves a little help, like you, and we get to keep doing our work.'

That explained the dark horse winners.

'Look around, kid! Nature isn't static, and it's always full of surprises. Take this cold front right now. Everyone comes into these races believing they just have to be strong and fast, that studying images of the terrain and digital maps is enough to know what they're going to get. It rarely is. You know that already from that glacier you and the other fellow had to climb.'

'You were there? Thought I saw someone.'

Mike nodded. 'You did, but it wasn't me. We've been watching from the start. That's how we know who to pick. We have to be careful, choose someone who could plausibly win. Now let's get back to the question at hand: do you want my help with that other calf? Do you want to win this race?'

Marmeg looked down at her cuff and her brothers' goofy smiles. She didn't have to tell them the whole story, but she did have to come home with some money. It was that or call her mother to come bail her out. That was the worst possibility Marmeg could imagine.

Amihan would never forgive Marmeg for the enormous sin of spending her money on gear and race fees. She would call it gambling. And she would be convinced that God was punishing Marmeg for partaking of such an evil pastime. She might be right, considering that Marmeg would be back to club security and nothing more if she didn't place. Winning by any means, even for half the prize money, would be better than that.

'Do it.'

Mike handed her a few white pills. 'These won't help with the pain now, but they will later.'

He went back to the trunk and pulled out a dark-brown glass bottle. He worked the cork out and handed Marmeg the bottle. She washed the pills down in one swallow, glad that Jeffy had given her opportunities to drink cheap booze. At least she didn't make a fool of herself by choking on whatever this was. It burned the back of her throat. A pleasant, tingling warmth soon spread through her body. She leaned her head back against the rough wood and closed her eyes.

'You go ahead and scream if you need to. Nobody's around to hear it.'

That sounded like a line in a bad horror vid. Marmeg chuckled, but she kept her eyes closed. The sounds of gear clinking played counterpoint to the pops and crackles from the wood stove. The scent of smoke filled the air. Marmeg sank into a stupor.

A sensation of cold and wet against her leg snapped her eyes open. Mike rubbed an alcohol pad against the old incision on her other calf.

'Ready?' he asked.

'As ever.'

Marmeg lay on her side and clenched her hands around the edge of the mattress. Mike sliced into her flesh, a quick, sure cut. She gritted her teeth against the pain; no screaming, not this time. She was breathing fast and harsh by the time he dug in with a pair of tweezers and extracted the bad chip. While he disinfected the replacement, she took a deep, steadying breath and reached for the brown glass bottle. She gulped three times.

'You better put that down before I finish this.'

He was much more deft with the capsule placement than she had been. She was surprised that he knew what to do. Unlike her field surgery, he took the time to close the wound neatly, wiping it clean before applying the glue. The result was a red, ragged mess, but it looked better than her other leg.

'I'm not going near the quad chips and your femoral artery.' He handed Marmeg her screen. 'Your turn.'

She pulled up the control software and reprogrammed the new capsules. She had splurged for a brainstem chip as her only legit surgery, using the programming contest money she had ferreted away from her mother. One of its benefits was that her muscles adapted more quickly to program changes. Another was that new chips would integrate faster with her physiology. The pain, however, was something she would have to ignore for the next twelve hours.

Marmeg hissed as she limped to the table where her gear pack lay open. She gritted her teeth, pulled the calf exos on, and went through a basic test sequence: walk, run in place, jump, balance on one foot. The incisions twinged but the pain intensity decreased with every flexion and extension of her muscles.

As a final exercise, Marmeg jumped from the floor on to the table, landing on it in a crouch and poised for her next motion. Mountain Mike leaned against the door, his arms crossed across his narrow chest, his expression inscrutable under the facial hair. His eyes followed her movements.

Marmeg leapt lightly off the table and repacked. She left the two quadriceps exos out. They wouldn't be worth much on the open market. She'd have plenty of time to replace them once she was done with this race, though she wouldn't have much money, not after she shared with the Mikes. That meant no license for Felix.

'What'll you do with your half?' she said, stowing the last of the gear.

'We use it to keep up the knowledge of how to live with the land. When catastrophe strikes, which it inevitably will, what are you embeds going to do? Your gear makes you dependent on technology. Same with everyone who never leaves the city. Without electricity and clean water and food delivered to you, you'll be lost. You'll need people like us to show you how to survive. Someone has to keep the old skills alive.'

Mike was busy at the stove, poking inside with a metal rod and splashing water into it from a bucket that Marmeg hadn't noticed before. The flames died down into glowing bits of wood and burnt black sections. He closed the stove door.

'We also use the money to maintain these cabins, pay for our phones, and supplement our food. This land can provide a lot, but we get hungry for cake and beer sometimes, too.' He grinned. His teeth were yellow but straight. 'Let's go.'

Marmeg followed him out of the cabin. Cold air struck her bare face. The sun had passed behind the western peaks, and icy rain had turned into flakes of snow. Marmeg's breath puffed out like a friendly ghost. She flicked on her cuff and checked their path. It wasn't taking them back to her original route.

'Where we heading?'

'Didn't you wonder how a bunch of survivalists like us could help you embeds win a race?'

'Wondered, yeah.'

'We've made tunnels under the ridges and built shortcuts through some of the passes as well. They're hidden from the satellites by plant cover. Nature does most of the work for us.'

Marmeg's conscience pricked her. Cheats were not looked on favourably in her neighbourhood, and Jeffy was especially contemptuous of people who didn't play fair. She hated the idea of lying to him. He'd supported her when she started fixing up embed gear. He'd slipped her money, shielded her from their mother's ire. Without him, she wouldn't be at this race today. She didn't want to let him down, but if she didn't place somewhere in the top five, she would disappoint everyone, especially herself.

Far behind them, thunder rumbled. They climbed up through the trees. The wind blew harder as the vegetation thinned out.

'I'm going to give you a new route,' Mike said.

He stopped at the base of a large slab of rock that rose like a wall. Marmeg craned her neck, following the vertical expanse until it vanished into the clouds. A snowflake landed in her slack-jawed mouth, a tiny crystal of cold that dissolved on her hot tongue.

Mike pulled an old-style handheld from his back pocket. Marmeg flicked on her cuff and allowed him to send her a file. It was a map overlay, much like the one she had made, but with a far more direct route.

"Nuf miles?'

'It'll be enough. Just don't hug the next racer you come across.'

'What?'

'That boy you helped over the ice field. I'm fairly certain he's the one who fried your chips. It was probably when you let him get close.'

'Zir,' Marmeg corrected automatically while her mind raced. Had Ardha been close enough to corrupt her chips? Yes: that final embrace. But zie had been so cooperative. *Stupid, stupid, stupid!* To fall for a pretty moot face and destroy her chance of winning this race fair and square. She wished she could smash Ardha's rating then and there, make sure no one trusted zir again.

Mike shrugged. 'Zie, he, she – until you change your genetics, you're still male or female as far as I'm concerned. You kids want to play at being something that you're not, that's between you. I'm not changing the way I talk.'

'Not playing,' Marmeg said irritably. 'Making waves. Changing the world. Better to judge on what you can do, not how you born. Bodies are going out. Nats be left behind.'

'You think so, eh? What do you expect will happen to the human species if we're all neutered embeds? Who's going to make the babies?' Mike shook his head. 'You think you're going to change the world. The reality is that the world is changing us. Pretty soon we're going to need all the *nat* skills and abilities that our ancestors had. I should know; I used to be like you, full of bits of silicon and titanium. I fought in the Congo. Nature is stronger than we give her credit for. Best that we learn to coexist peacefully with her.'

Not only was Mike a nat, he was a converted one – the

worst kind when it came to preaching – but his words didn't convince her. Companies like Minerva specialized in physical enhancements, but others were working on deeper changes. They wouldn't need babies in the future. They would live forever, bodies enhanced, minds uploaded.

Mike looked at her and sighed. 'Every year I try, hoping that the message gets through to someone...someday. You think you understand the world by seeing it through the grid, but reality is messier than bits and bytes.'

They'd been walking along the base of the massive rock wall. Mike stopped at a cluster of scraggly bushes growing between some rocks. He pushed the branches aside and rolled a couple stones away, revealing an opening that was half Marmeg's height and as wide as an arm span.

'You'll see for yourself when you're older. Here's the tunnel. Someone will meet you when you need to get into the next one.'

'This? Be a tunnel?'

Mike grinned. 'I never said you could run it. Trust me, you'll crawl through just fine. In fact, your calves are going to thank you while you're on your knees. It's too bad you lost the upper leg enhancements, but this will still save you a lot of time.'

He took something out of his pocket and then stretched it over Marmeg's head.

'It's a head lamp. The switch is here, on top. Good luck. I'm going to cover the entrance once you're in, so don't try to turn back.'

Marmeg looked at him like he was crazy, which he was, and then decided that she was equally crazy to do this. She got down on hands and knees, turned on the lamp, and went in.

———

The crawl went on and on until Marmeg's arms, legs and back ached. She felt like it lasted for hours, but according to her cuff, it only took forty-five minutes. The sky was nearly dark by the time she emerged into another cluster of bushes and rocks.

She looked around but saw no one. She pushed rocks across the hole and tried to arrange the bushes to hide it from a casual glance. The task was harder than it looked.

After three attempts to make it seem natural, Marmeg shrugged and gave up. Let the Mountain Mikes make it better if they wanted to.

She loaded the map from Mike, oriented herself, and walked in the direction it indicated. As she moved, the kinks in her body relaxed into a minor nuisance. She tried jogging and then running. Jumping didn't work as well as it had with the quad exos, but at least the pain from her cuts faded to a dull ache. She could maintain a respectable pace.

Snow dusted the ground like powdered sugar on cinnamon cake. Marmeg's stomach growled. Her throat felt parched. The booze back at the cabin couldn't have helped with hydration. She opened her mouth and caught a few snowflakes on her tongue. They melted with a sensation like popping bubbles.

A laugh burst from her. She wished Felix were there. Lee and Jeffy, too. None of them had left the city, seen true wilderness. Here, with nothing but trees and snow, sky above, dirt below, Marmeg's spirit soared with glee. It had all gone to shit without a pot, but she was *there*. She was experiencing something that none of her family could comprehend, surrounded as they were by cement and glass.

Marmeg ran faster, breathing hard and enjoying the burn of cold air in her lungs. The incisions on her calves tugged with each step, but the sensation was gentle and far removed. Snow blurred into an almost uniform whiteness. She had to land each step by feel and hope her balance held. A trickle of sweat traced the space between her shoulder blades. Fingers and toes warmed as her blood pulsed and breath deepened.

'I'm alive!' Marmeg yelled into the dark expanse above.

She'd left the head lamp on. She slowed to a jog and switched it off, then activated the night vision in her contact lenses. Marmeg ran until she saw another massive slab of granite looming ahead. The time on her cuff showed nearly ten o'clock. She'd been out for eleven hours.

Her mileage showed as forty-five, far more than she'd expected. GPS access had been blocked inside the tunnel, so the routing software that Minerva required had extrapolated from the terrain. It calculated the miles as if she'd climbed over rather than crawled through. How had the Mountain Mikes found that loophole?

She arrived near the base of the mountain and couldn't go farther. The map indicated that she should turn left. Five minutes later, a figure loomed out of the darkness, its hooded face wrapped in a giant woolly scarf.

'This way,' rumbled a low, decidedly male voice.

Marmeg looked for a beard, but it was impossible to find in the swaddled head, especially with her night vision on. The Mike said nothing more as he revealed the tunnel. He stayed silent even after she went in.

The light from the head lamp blinded her when she turned it on. Marmeg blinked and squinted until her pupils adjusted, then began the long, painful crawl to the other side. Muscles cooled, breath slowed, and a deep cold seeped into her body from the rock surrounding her.

This tunnel was considerably longer than the previous one and had some uphill and downhill sections. Halfway through an incline, the pain pills began to wear off. She couldn't get into the pack for more, so she gritted her teeth and kept moving. Her calves were screaming with pain by the time she came out of the other end. It was nearly midnight. All of the elation from earlier had evaporated.

Marmeg stopped to stretch her pain-wracked body. She popped a couple more stims and three pain pills into her mouth and tried to work up some spit. The mass went down in a painful, bitter lump that made her gag. The analgesics would take some time to work, but the stimulants were fast.

She sat and waited for them to hit. She hated this race. Winning by any means, cheating the GPS system, getting help – and for what? So she could give half the prize money to a group of people whose values meant nothing to her. This race was supposed to be her chance to prove herself, to prove that she could compete with those who had the latest and greatest tech. Now she was like every other lowlife filcher.

She ignored the rules, broke laws, and stomped on anyone who stood in her way.

She checked her cuff. The mileage had jumped by another fifteen. That put her total at sixty miles with only fifteen more to go. If all her gear still worked, she could match her earlier four-miles-per-hour pace. She could finish the race and beat the record. Unless that, too, was faked.

Marmeg groaned and hit the ground with a fist. The faces of her brothers stared at her from the cuff.

'What should I do, Jeffy?'

The image was still, silent, accusatory.

You started this, it seemed to say. *Finish it! Don't be a whiny little girl. You've already done enough to be disqualified. You might as well go for the kill.*

Marmeg shuddered with cold. Too much time sitting still. Her calves stung at the incisions. She could feel warm blood as it seeped through the bandages and froze against the frigid air. Would bloody ice crystals look like rubies?

Red gems dripped from her legs and fell to the ground, forming a carpet around her. The crystals caught the starlight, sparked with their own internal fire. A thousand tiny flames surrounded Marmeg with their warmth.

She woke with a start. The forest was black. Nothing but chilled dirt and melting snow lay beneath her.

'Wake up,' she told herself, slapping her cheeks.

Her cuff said she'd been asleep for twenty minutes, and her body felt heavy from the weight of it. The stim pills had begun their work, though. With a soft groan, Marmeg stood and forced herself to walk, step by slow, dull step.

A quick check showed the leg exos and one remaining sleeve functioning correctly. The heating elements on the torso shell remained broken – no surprise – but the heart and lung monitors read correctly, and the abdominal boosters were doing their job. So, why couldn't she move faster?

You're tired.

She put one foot in front of the next, following the path set out for her. What else could she do? Around one o'clock, the moon rose above the eastern peaks. Its light showed breaks in the cloud cover. Marmeg couldn't see the stars she'd hoped for, but the moonbeams made for better company than the storm-clouded blackness. The snow had stopped falling. The ground crunched under her steps and glimmered from the faint light.

The pain pills started kicking in, and Marmeg picked up her pace. No matter what prize money she won, she wouldn't be out for another solitary moonlit hike any time soon. She'd caught a snowflake on her tongue. She'd heard ice crackle under her boots, mimicking the sound of broken glass that had been stepped on too many times. Or the sound facial bones made when your mom's boyfriend didn't much like your mom's kid.

She wished she could have a do-over, a second chance to prove that she was as good as the legit embeds and moots; that she could beat them at their own game; that she deserved to be at a university with people who were born licensed, who never had to worry about food or medicine or shots. But that kind of thinking trapped her in the dark corners of her mind, where bad ideas looped infinitely.

Maybe Mountain Mike was right. Life was never fair. Winning by cheating was okay if you used the money for the right reasons. In her case, she wanted to buy little Felix's license so he could get his shots and go to school. She wanted a full degree, which ultimately meant a better life for her and her family. Those goals were noble enough to let the ends justify the means, weren't they?

A figure loomed up out of the darkness. Marmeg gasped and nearly lost her footing. She stumbled to a halt a few feet away, breathing hard. When she looked at the person, she saw a face hidden under bushy hair that glinted in the moonlight.

'The hell?' Marmeg demanded, heart hammering.

'No tunnels for miles yet!'

'You're this girl? The one with the leg cuts and all?' The muffled voice was high-pitched.

Marmeg peered at the Mountain Mike. 'You a lady?'

The bundle of hair nodded. 'We wear beards to fool the cameras. As long as we don't come too far into the open, they can't tell us apart. Follow me.'

'But –'

'Come on!'

Marmeg bit back an irritated reply. This Mike ploughed straight through the underbrush. Marmeg followed, small branches smacking into the backs of her calves and making the incisions sting. Her cuff said she'd been on the correct path to the next tunnel. Now they headed toward an overland route that she'd considered before the race. It was direct, but it required rock climbing skills and equipment that she didn't have.

They arrived at a tumble of boulders. Mountain Mike scrambled up on her hands and knees. Marmeg decided that she might as well take it easy and use all four limbs too. There wasn't much point in jumping like a goat when she had no idea where to go. What would they put her through next?

A light breeze blew over them and grew stronger as they climbed higher. Broken clouds outlined by ghostly white moonlight hung behind the ridge's saw-toothed silhouette. As she and Mike neared the top, the wind blew so hard that they were forced to lean into it. The bare rock was mostly free of snow and ice, though a few wind-sheltered pockets glittered like treasure. She scooped a handful into her mouth. Only a few drops of cold liquid, but the relief to her throat was immeasurable.

Mountain Mike tapped her on the shoulder and then pointed down – into the wind and a steep, rocky slope. She put her bristly face next to Marmeg's ear, and Marmeg fought the urge to pull away.

'There's someone down there who's hurt. Another contestant. I think you might be able to help me with him. Follow me very carefully. He went down this scree and got trapped under a rockfall. I don't want the same thing to happen to us.'

Marmeg peered down, trying to see the other person. The nearer rocks reflected the moon's glow, but nothing else was visible. Her attention locked on to her footing once they transitioned to the down slope. Stones littered the ground, ranging in size from pebbles to boulders wider than her arm span. Each step sent a few of them skittering away. The rattle reminded her of gunfire, a sound that accompanied many nights at home.

Mountain Mike was doing a respectable job of the climb, though she ended up on her ass after half of her steps. Marmeg managed to keep her balance. The lack of full leg exos made the job more difficult than it should have been. She wondered how another race contestant had screwed this up.

Then she saw the massive vertical scar of pale grey against darker rock. At its base lay a jumble of boulders, and under that, the lower half of a body. She winced and turned away for a second, imagining what it must feel like to be crushed beneath that kind of weight. Her legs would be pulp.

Marmeg and Mike inched sideways, perpendicular to the slope, until they stood near the injured contestant. One look at the pale, unconscious face and Marmeg identified zir as Ardha. *You got what you deserved*, said the vengeful part of Marmeg's mind. *Shut up. Nobody deserves this*, said another.

Marmeg bent to lift a rock from Ardha's body.

'No!' Mike said. 'Don't touch those rocks! I don't know how stable they are, and they're saving his life right now by keeping him from bleeding out.'

'What you want from me, then?'

'I want you to enable his grid access. That way the race organizers or his support team will know he's in trouble. They'll come get his body, and you can keep going.'

Marmeg shook her head. 'Can't do.'

'Why not? We'll make sure you still place. Don't worry about that.'

'Can't. Not *won't*. Can't access zir cuff.'

'But you're a hacker.' Mountain Mike sounded confused.

'Not so easy. Could hack it, yeah, but takes time. Like hours time, not minutes time.'

Mike blew out a frustrated breath and carefully sat down next to Ardha's body. She held a hand on zir wrist, checking zir pulse, Marmeg guessed. Then Mike felt Ardha's forehead and cheeks. She reached into a pocket, pulled out an old phone, and held it up to her head.

'His pulse is weak, and he's clammy,' she said, speaking into the handset.

Marmeg could barely hear the words over the wind.

'Maybe another hour or so to live, best guess. Not long enough for her to run to the finish line and inform them.' A pause. 'No, that won't work. What story could she give them?' A longer pause, then louder: 'Are you kidding? Just leave him here?'

Mike snapped the phone closed in anger and stood. 'If you idiots didn't think you were invincible, you wouldn't get us into situations like this. Let's go!'

'What about zir?'

'We have to leave him. You need to win this race more than we need to help him. So says our leadership. He lives or dies on his support team. That's a risk all of you take, right? You sign the damn waivers when you enter.'

'Nobody's ever died.'

'Then he won't either. Now, come on!'

'No.'

'What do you mean?'

'Not leaving zir. Not like this.'

Mike flapped her arms like she was trying to fly off the mountain. 'I thought you said you couldn't do anything?'

'Got my own grid access.'

'You can't use that. Then we all lose. We'll get nothing for helping you, and once they realize you've been working with us, they'll ban you from races forever. Is that what you want?'

Marmeg was certainly happy to see Ardha lose the race after what zie had done to her. But to potentially let a person die over money? She would despise herself for it.

She'd pulled herself from the precipice of self-hatred once before, when the glow of being a prodigy had worn off. Marmeg had lived the high-school party circuit for a year. Jeffy left for the service, and she had no one to remind her of her worth. Contest money that Amihan didn't take was burned on pills. Spare time – and she had plenty of that – was lost in the haze of self-loathing.

If she hadn't met T'shawn, if he hadn't remembered Marmeg from the old days, she might never have crawled out of her head hole and back into life. This race, the prize money, her dream future: none of these was worth the risk of returning to that ugly corner of her mind.

'Race not the be-all. Zie might die.'

'I know. That's why I brought you here. Look, this situation is crap, but we have to put the greater good first. If you won't change your mind...well, I can't blame you, but I can't help you, either.'

She turned and started walking up the scree.

'That's it?' Marmeg called after her. 'Buncha nats think

you're the stuff! Let a kid die on money? Some things not worth being.'

Marmeg took out her screen, enabled her grid access, and sent a message to the race organizers. She took some photos of Ardha's situation, too – so they'd know what to bring – and sent a capture of her map with the GPS coordinates displayed. She made sure to disable her grid access again after seeing the send confirmation.

Minerva Corporation did good work. Maybe they'd be decent and not disqualify her for trying to save another contestant's life. They could check her system log for proof – she accessed the grid only to help Ardha.

'Better live, asshole,' Marmeg whispered to the unmoving body. Ardha's face was beautiful in spite of its half-bloodied, pale state.

She stood, flexed her calves, and ran up the rocky slope. Pebbles flew behind her, drawn by gravity to whatever waited at the bottom. The Mike's figure was a shadow crawling along the scree and struggling for purchase. Marmeg continued her swift ascent without giving it a second look.

———

Marmeg got enough of a lead on Mountain Mike that she was well out of sight before taking her bearings. Once she had her location, she pulled up her original route. It was only two miles away, which wasn't bad considering how completely she had put herself in the hands of the Mikes.

The moon shone overhead. The clouds had fractured into

patches of fluffy grey across the sky. Stars twinkled in the gaps, crystal clear even with the lunar glare for competition. Hundreds of diamond pinpoints – more than Marmeg had ever seen. Cold settled into her, a now-familiar friend, and her spirits lightened.

Win or lose, she'd made the only right decision. Losing wouldn't be so bad. Then she wouldn't have to share the contest money with people who valued an agenda over a human being. Or maybe they were only indifferent when an embed's life was at risk. What would they have said if it had been a Mike under the crush of rock? How many Mikes died out there with no one the wiser?

The land felt emptier with that last thought. Running into Ardha the first time had been a coincidence. If the Mountain Mikes hadn't sought her out, she might have finished the race without seeing anyone else. The lack of humanity was strange, like an empty street with no cop cars to explain it – wrong but not frightening.

Marmeg's cuff alerted her to the upcoming pass. This one would take her to the finish line. She found the trail marked by cairns and followed it up an uneven set of steps carved out of the granite mountainside. The footing wasn't difficult, but she chafed at having to climb the steps rather than simply leaping up them. That would have required functional thigh-control chips.

She walked between looming masses of rock. The faintest trace of purplish blue coloured the eastern sky. She checked her cuff: three-thirty in the morning. The sun would rise in two hours, but she would reach the finish line long before then.

The rushing noise of Rainbow Falls told her she was close. Next came fences made of rough wood to guide people and keep them on the trail, away from the cliff. And then, at last, the striated columns of Devils Postpile rose into the sky. Artificial lights illuminated the natural formation, a beacon to the contestants: the end of the race.

The thrum of an electric generator greeted Marmeg as she loped into the staging area. She squinted against the flood of light triggered by her motion. Drone-cams perched on tree branches. The nearest ones launched and pointed their lenses at her. Zippered tents littered the area. Silhouettes stirred inside some of them, probably alerted by their drones.

Marmeg flicked on her cuff and saw that it was three minutes past four o'clock. She hadn't beaten the record. Apparently, no one else had either, given the lack of a welcoming committee. A shadowy figure emerged from the trees on the far side of the camp and walked toward her. Zie came into the lit area, and Marmeg recognized the blond moot from the registration booth.

'I'm so sorry,' zie said. 'I had to, you know, answer the call of nature. So, you're the first! Congratulations on winning this year's race!'

The drone-cams buzzed closer, recording and transmitting the conversation. Marmeg attempted a smile as they walked to a nondescript brown tent.

Zie unzipped the opening and called into it, 'Jer, wake up! We have a winner.'

Within minutes, all the tents had opened. People and drones spilled out into the darkness. Groggy journos snapped pictures of Marmeg. She waved away their questions while she ate an energy bar and huddled in a scratchy blanket someone handed her.

Meanwhile, the blond – whose name turned out to be Larlou – and Jer were rapidly setting up the official Minerva booth. Ten minutes after Marmeg's arrival, the second race contestant ran in. Keni Matsuki, last year's third-place winner, held an arm swathed in bloody smartskin. The medical team immediately looked to zir injury.

Marmeg's tired mind snapped to attention at the sight of blood.

'Hey, Larlou,' she said. 'Ardha – zie okay?'

Larlou looked up from the equipment rack.

'Who? What are you talking about?'

'Ardha! Sent you a message. Zie was hurt bad.'

Larlou looked at Jer in bewilderment. 'Did you hear about this from any of the support teams?'

'No,' Jer said. He frowned and turned to Marmeg. 'You said you pinged them?'

'Not them. You. Message to race org.'

'Well, shit, kid, why didn't you inform zir support team?'

'Didn't know their address. Why didn't you get my message?'

'I see it now,' Larlou said. 'Zie looks bad. We weren't expecting anything urgent, so we weren't looking at messages. I'll go find zir team's tent.'

'Zie doesn't make it, it's on you.'

She closed her eyes against a surge of frustration and fear. So much time had elapsed. What if they were too late? She had assumed that Ardha would be taken care of and gone by the time she arrived. Stupid and selfish not to ask about zir condition sooner.

'Wait a minute,' Jer said.

Marmeg opened her heavy eyelids.

'You sent us a message. That means you accessed grid data.'

She nodded. 'Had to. Zie was unconscious. Couldn't access through zir cuff. Turned mine off after sending.'

Jer's pale lips pressed into a thin line.

Marmeg's blood surged in anger. 'What? Was I wrong? Leave zir to die out there?'

Her stomach sank at Jer's expression. They'd declared her the winner. Would they take it back? Could they? Most of her wanted nothing more than a hot shower and a soft bed, but her sense of justice couldn't rest. Minerva had to do the right thing, make the compassionate call. Didn't they?

Jer walked away, murmuring into his cuff. Dawn had arrived in full effect. Marmeg could see his lips move, but she couldn't read the words. Adrenaline, pills, pain-induced endorphins: all of them crashed with the break of day. The energy to worry or rage evaporated. She collapsed into the blanket on the ground and fell asleep.

When she woke, rays of sunlight shone through the tree branches at a steep angle. Dust motes danced in the beams, and the aroma of frying eggs, bacon, and pancakes filled the air. She breathed in deeply and stretched. The cuts in her calves tugged uncomfortably, reminding Marmeg that she needed to see the medics.

The site swarmed with people. Contestants, supporters,

and journos stood everywhere, eating and talking. Drone cameras buzzed in any available air space. Someone must have noticed that Marmeg was awake, because several cams moved to circle above her, swooping down to near face level and being annoying. Worse, three actual people surrounded her.

'How does it feel?' one of them asked.

'Congratulations! And condolences,' said another. 'For what it's worth, plenty of people on the grid think you did the right thing.'

'What?' Marmeg said stupidly. Her brain felt like it was filled with wet beach sand.

The journos exchanged glances.

'You came in first place, but they've disqualified you because you accessed the grid. Keni Matsuki is the official winner.'

'Oh.'

'Aren't you upset? It's looking very likely that you saved...' the journo checked zir cuff '...Ardhanara Jagadisha's life. People are already circulating a petition on your behalf to get Minerva to reinstate you as the winner.'

'Oh. Thanks.'

Marmeg walked past the baffled journos and over to the race tent.

'Truth?' she said to Larlou and Jer.

They looked at her apologetically.

'The race committee disqualified you, Mary. I'm so sorry,' Larlou said. 'I think you did the right thing, but they're saying that we can't know if you accessed any information or talked to someone who might have helped you while you were online.'

Marmeg hadn't done either of those, but she had taken help from people off the grid. She had cheated. How could she justify defending the win?

'Look, kid,' Jer said, 'you did your best and you did great, but you should've hurried back here instead of turning on your access. We didn't know about Ardhanara until then anyway. Zie was alive when we picked zir up. Everyone knows the risk they're taking when they enter this race. Zie did too, and frankly, the route zie picked wasn't smart. What you did was noble, but it wasn't too smart, either.'

'Jer!' Larlou protested. 'Don't listen to him. If there's enough public outcry, Minerva will force the race committee to change its mind. It'll all come out right, Mary. You'll see. Have some faith.'

Words bubbled into Marmeg's mind and floated away before she could speak. Was it better to confess the truth or play the wronged innocent? She had broken the rules – not the ones the race people knew about, but rules nonetheless. At least Ardha had survived. Marmeg hoped zie felt like an ass when zie found out who had saved zir.

'Is there anything we can do for you?' Larlou said. 'Your support team never showed.'

'That's because she doesn't have one,' Jer said. His voice wasn't entirely unkind. 'I bet I know what she needs.'

Jer reached for Marmeg's cuff hand. She pulled it back by instinct.

'I'm going to transfer some credit,' Jer said patiently. He looked sad. 'I wish it had turned out differently, but this race is as much a publicity event for Minerva as it is any real test of ability. You handed them an excuse to keep you out of the winner's circle. They're going to take that as a gift.'

Shame and anger welled in Marmeg until she wanted to scream. Instead, she thrust out her cuff while looking away at the treetops. She needed money to get home. Taking it from Jer was better than having to call Jeffy or her mother.

'Thanks,' she mumbled, reactivating grid access on her screen so the transaction could complete.

The amount would cover bus fare and some frugal meals. Messages cascaded in as the cuff and screen rediscovered the rest of the world. Marmeg watched as the number ticked up and then jumped and then shot toward the moon. The cuff's buffer overflowed first, then her screen's. Marmeg muttered a curse she'd learned from Felix and Lee's father.

She searched the grounds for a speck of privacy to read them, but a few persistent drones wouldn't stop chasing her. She glared up at them.

'Did right!' she said loudly but not shouting.

If she was acting for the grid, she would rather play for sympathy. And she spoke the truth. Abandoning her message queue, she sat down in the middle of everything, activity swirling around her. She had yet to take off her gear.

Marmeg gritted her teeth against a groan when she pulled off the first calf exo. She couldn't help but wince. Someone must have noticed, because a medic was on her by the time she had the second one off.

The medic took one look at her blood-crusted pants and motioned Marmeg to follow. Her legs were little better than jelly without the exos. She stumbled on nothing, and the medic reached out, supporting her by the elbow the rest of the way. Pitying looks accompanied them as they walked. The relative isolation of the tent provided her with much-needed privacy.

'What the hell did you do?' the medic demanded. 'It looks like you cut yourself open with a kitchen knife.'

'Near as much. Had to swap fried chips.'

The medic looked horrified. 'Out there? By yourself? With no sterilization or anaesthesia? You're insane!' Zie shook zir head. 'You're lucky you made it this long.'

Zie kept muttering about infection and poisoning as zie readied a tray of gleaming instruments.

'Lie down,' zie said. 'On your stomach.'

Marmeg yelped as chilly fingers pushed around her incisions.

'Oh, please. It must've hurt a lot more when you made these incisions. I can see quite a bit of swelling here, but the wound is closed. We're better off leaving it alone. I'm going to take some blood samples to check for infection.'

Marmeg craned her head and watched the medic draw a vial of blood. Zie placed a few drops into a row of cylinders the size of her thumb. After a minute, zie scanned each one with a handheld and frowned at the screen. Marmeg held her breath until the medic's face relaxed.

'Lucky girl. Your blood is clear of sepsis. You do have a mild infection, which is hardly unexpected, but it's nothing a course of antibiotics won't clear up. I'm going to get them from the supply box outside. Stay put.'

Marmeg sat up. The world spun. She debated getting a few more stim pills from her backpack, but the medic returned before she'd moved. Zie carried a blister pack of antibiotics and a bottle of water.

'Take two now and another one every twelve hours until they're all gone. And no more stimulants.' Had zie read her mind? 'You need to let your body rest and recover. Get lots of sleep, drink plenty of water, and take it easy on the legs for at least a week. No exos! I recommend seeing a surgeon at that point to reopen your calves and check the capsule placement. They might be able to reduce the scarring, too. As it is now, you're going to end up with some ugly ones.'

Marmeg sighed and took the first dose. The giant, bitter pills stuck in her throat, and she drank nearly half the bottle before she swallowed them.

'Thanks.'

'You're welcome. I'm sorry about the race.'

'Same.'

She shouldered her pack and brought up her planned return route on her cuff. A free shuttle would get her to Mammoth Lakes. From there she could catch the bus to Los Angeles.

A winding cement path led to a rectangular building and the signpost for the shuttle. There was nowhere to sit while waiting, so Marmeg dropped her pack on the pavement and slumped beside it. Two journo drones had trailed her, but they lost interest once she stopped moving. She had thirty minutes until the next shuttle. In her sleep-deprived state, it felt like an eternity.

The bus pulled in with a squeal of brakes that woke her from a light doze. A couple and two young children got down, and Marmeg climbed on. She took up two seats, one for herself and another for the pack, but it didn't matter. The bus was empty except for her.

She dozed off again, rousing only when the driver informed her that they'd arrived in town. She could smell toasted bread as she stepped off. Her stomach growled. Marmeg entered the bakery from which the lovely, mouth-watering odours came, and ordered a bagel, toast with fried eggs, and a pitcher of orange juice. It would make a sizeable dent in the money Jer had given her.

She sat at a table in the back corner, though there was no one to hide from except the server. The food arrived steaming. It was the most delectable meal of Marmeg's life, and she devoured it at a pace that barely allowed for chewing and swallowing.

'Glad you enjoyed your meal,' the server said as zie cleared the dishes away.

'Best ever.' Marmeg held up her cuff to pay.

'No charge.'

'What?'

The server smiled. 'Most everyone here follows the race. A free breakfast is the least I can do.'

'Thanks.'

Win or lose, fame had its benefits. Marmeg made sure to bump the server's and the bakery's ratings on her way out.

The bus terminal in town was small, but it was enclosed and clean, and had padded seats. Marmeg slept until her cuff zapped her awake. Time to catch the bus. She blearily joined the handful of others getting on. The driver stopped her when she held her cuffed wrist to the credit scanner.

'Sorry, cash only today. Scanner's broken.'

'Jokin'?'

The driver shook his head. 'There's a cash dispenser inside. I'll wait for you.'

Marmeg kept her pack with her and limped back into the station. She swiped her cuff three times at the machine to no effect. Then she noticed the small card with OUT OF ORDER scribbled in red and taped to the top.

'My God, why hast thou forsaken me?' she muttered, feeling a strong urge to kick the machine.

She walked back out and asked the driver if he knew of any other machines nearby. He didn't. When was the next bus? Not for two more days. His face crinkled with pity.

'I'll make you a deal,' he said. 'Show me the credit balance on your cuff. If it's enough, I'll give you a ride. You can get me some cash at the next station.'

'Deal,' Marmeg agreed.

She sat and put the pack vertically next to herself. She leaned against it like an old friend and fell into a deep sleep. In her dreams, towering trees tangled with walls of granite. Rocks crashed through them, creating an avalanche of roots and soil and mangled, screaming bodies.

'Hey,' said a gentle voice. 'Got to wake up here and get your bus fare.'

Marmeg awoke disoriented and stared at the owner of the voice: a greying man with asphalt-coloured skin. Right. She was on a bus, nearly out of money, and going home a cheat and a failure. *You're wrong, Ma. God doesn't love me.*

Every muscle ached and every joint protested when she stood and pulled on the pack. The first four steps along the bus aisle were pure agony. Then blood pulsed its way to the right places, including her brain. She wondered where they were until she saw the sign proclaiming RIDGECREST in faded green lettering. The cash machine looked even worse. At least it dispensed.

Marmeg was tempted by the smell of coffee but decided it would be smarter to sleep. She thought of all the messages on her cuff. At the very least, she owed a note to Jeffy that she'd made it on to the bus in one piece. Then again, if the race news kept topping the feeds, he would know enough.

'Hoy. You Mary Guinto, right? Graf me?' said a voice from behind her.

She turned and saw two kids, probably thirteen or fourteen years old. One had her screen thrust out at Marmeg. Her face had a shy, nervous expression that felt all too familiar.

'Lost the race.'

'Won it, squares!' said the kid fiercely. 'They gone it 'cause of who you be, but we all know you done first.'

Marmeg smiled at her defenders. 'Okay. I'll graf.'

She scribbled a message next to her signature: TO MY FIRST FANS. Her pack felt a little lighter on her way back to the bus.

Marmeg's cuff bleated as she took her seat. She flicked it on. The backlog had grown. One after another, messages scrolled by. The earliest were congratulatory. They became supportive, then outraged. Petitions against Minerva's race committee were filed. Many protested that it was blatant discrimination against a postnatal licensee. Others were appalled by Minerva's inhumanity.

Hours' worth of drama played out in the space of a few minutes. Her ratings had soared, dipped, risen, and dipped again. They had acquired a life of their own.

She set her cuff not to wake her until the bus arrived in Los Angeles. Of the rest of the journey, she remembered nothing, not even her dreams.

Marmeg felt more like herself when she stepped off the bus at the dingy LA station. A gentle mist fell from a cement-coloured sky. The sun had set, painting the west an angry orange.

She walked past the lot full of two-seater pods and older electric cars, intending to foot it to the nearest train station. The sight of her family's rusty electric minivan caught her off guard. Dirty beads of water trickled down its side windows. Marmeg peered in and saw with a sinking heart that her mother sat at the wheel. The window glass retracted jerkily into the door.

'Come in out of the rain, mahal.'

Marmeg slung her pack into the middle row and climbed into the passenger seat.

'How'd you know?'

'Oh, honey, you're all over the feeds. I made Jeffy tell me how you were planning to get home, so I've been waiting here. I'm off today.'

'Ma, that's...real nice of you. Thanks.'

Amihan patted Marmeg's left hand. 'Least I could do for my girl after all she's put herself through.'

'No stink?'

'No stink. I'm not mad at you. Everybody makes mistakes. Lord knows, I get that better than most, eh?' Amihan laughed. 'Sometimes, we have to learn the hard way, us women, especially in our family.'

The wiper blades squeaked, and the scent of stale tobacco filled the car. Marmeg's comfort at being home warred with her mother's unexpected sympathy. When added to everything else that had happened in the past twenty-four hours, the whole world felt off-kilter.

She stared through the window at a city turned upside down by a hundred perfect water drops. She was a snowflake poised on a warm tongue, awaiting its inevitable death and cherishing the memory of its brief, spectacular life.

Reality crashed in: familiar shop fronts with peeling paint and screen signs with half their pixels gone. This part of the neighbourhood was etched into Marmeg's memory as clearly as traces on a circuit board.

'What we doing here?'

Amihan kept her gaze fixed on the wet, shiny blackness of the road.

'Ma? Talk to me!'

Her mother pulled into a cracked, weed-choked driveway alongside an industrial-looking building. CASA FRANCISCA WOMEN'S SHELTER: the sign hung on the wall in dull metal letters. Amihan turned off the car's engine.

'Tell me the truth. Did you register and pay for the nursing home programme?'

'No.'

'Did you spend that money on the race?'

'It's my money.'

'Did you?'

'Yes.'

'Thank you for being honest. Tonight, I'm going to take you home. Your brothers have planned a little party, and I don't want to disappoint them. Tomorrow morning, you can come here on your own, or I'll drop you off on the way to work. You will not be welcome at home again until you figure out how to fix this mess.'

'Fix it your way?'

'Seems better than yours.'

'I won the race!'

'And they took it away from you, like I knew they would. You think because you're smart, you can engineer your way into their life, but you'll never be one of them. They don't want people like us messing up their perfect circles.'

Marmeg crossed her arms, restrained herself against the urge to smash something. Anything.

Amihan reached out a tentative hand. 'Take your hardships with grace, Mary Margaret. God is testing you! This is your chance to earn His forgiveness.'

'And yours?'

'Mine comes through His grace. I'm your mother, so I'll always love you, but I won't sit by and watch my daughter destroy her life. Are we clear?'

'Crystal.'

Amihan backed out of the driveway. They drove to the apartment in silence and left the van parked between a two-seater and an ancient gas-burner. The mist had turned to actual falling drops of rain. They hurried inside, where they were surprised by two boys in handmade party hats. A sign reading WELCOME HOME SISSY was written in wiggly lettering.

'Surprise!' shouted Lee and Felix, jumping up and down with giant grins plastered on their faces.

Marmeg forced a smile. She dropped her pack near the door and scooped her little brothers into a tight hug. Felix's sweet curls tickled her chin.

'Best brothers in the world,' she exclaimed, fighting tears.

'Hey, what about me?' Jeffy said, walking into the apartment.

Marmeg turned and gave Jeffy the next hug. His stubbly cheeks were cold and damp, and he held a bottle in each hand.

'Wine, Jeffy?' Amihan spoke in an appraising tone. She took the bottles from him and peered at the labels. 'This one's not bad,' she said. She walked to the kitchen and grabbed the corkscrew that lay on the countertop. The surface was so littered with pans and dishes that Marmeg could barely see the yellowing, cracked tiles underneath.

Amihan poured the wine into plastic cups and handed one each to Marmeg and Jeffy. She grabbed cans of soda from the fridge for Lee and Felix. Little eyes went wide.

'I get a whole can?' Felix squeaked.

'Sure, baby. We're celebrating!' Amihan said.

'We are? I got the wine to make Marm feel better for losing the race.'

'Jeffy! No, we're celebrating that Mary is coming to her senses and quitting this embed nonsense.'

Jeffy and Felix simultaneously said, 'She is?'

Jeffy looked at Marmeg for confirmation, and she shrugged. His face darkened.

'No way, Ma. We can't let her quit. She won! Do you know how hard that is?'

'But she didn't keep the win, and she threw away her future in the process.'

'Are you saying she should've let that person die?'

'Of course not, Jeffy. What do you take me for?'

'Enough! Too tired to fight this tonight,' Marmeg said. 'Sort it in daylight, brud, okay?' She raised her cup toward Jeffy, who glowered but raised his as well. 'To new beginnings.'

The first sip of wine left Marmeg's tongue coated in acid. The next slurp was as cool and sweet as a mountain stream. Whether or not she had deserved any of it – Ardha's sabotage, the Mikes' help, the disqualification – it didn't matter anymore. Nobody in real life got what they deserved. At least Marmeg had been spared the self-loathing she would've felt for winning by cheating.

Who was she kidding? She desperately wanted all of that success. She wanted to be out there, under the trees and the shadow of mountains, getting interviewed by journos and fending off sponsors and rabid fan requests. Instead, she stuffed some basics into her pack while the boys jumped away their soda high. Jeffy and their mother were too drunk to notice.

The celebration didn't last long. The younger boys sugar-crashed and turned in. Jeffy fell asleep on the sofa, and Amihan wept at the kitchen table about her ill-fated family until she passed out with her head on her arms.

Marmeg slung the pack over her shoulder. She stood by the door and took in the tableau. Better to leave now than face the drama of the morning. She ducked out and closed the door. The chill, moist air was a welcome relief after the stuffiness of their apartment. The rain had tapered into a heavy mist that clung to Marmeg and slicked the sidewalk. Fog blew in ghostly drifts from the coast and wove around the street lights.

A quarter of the distance passed before her calves protested. Too late she recalled the medic's warning to stay off her legs. She gritted her teeth against the pain, but she was limping badly by the time she arrived at the shelter.

'I'm sorry I don't have a bed for you,' said the night manager. She handed Marmeg a ratty sleeping bag. 'The rain's got us full tonight. You're welcome to find a spot on the floor.'

Marmeg found an empty space by the wall of a cavernous room lined with bunk beds, all occupied. She settled her pack behind her, trying to get the softer items to provide some cushion from the gear. Somewhere on the other side of the wall, a baby wailed. Marmeg slid her legs into the bag, shoes and all, and leaned back to check her ratings.

Minerva had released a statement saying they would look into the Sierra Challenge results, but as of yet, they hadn't contacted Marmeg even once. The only people who had reached out to her were others in similar situations: born without a license, filching their gear, stuck in dead-end jobs that didn't require legit schooling – the people for whom she embodied hope.

Her ratings bounded around like a demented basketball. She sighed as she cleared the cuff's message buffer again and again. In the final cluster of private messages was one from Jeffy: MOM'S WAITING AT BUS STATION FOR YOU. Too bad she hadn't seen the warning earlier. Then, near the end of the list, a one-liner from a meaningless address: SILENCE IS GOLDEN.

So, the Mountain Mikes were paying attention. Was that a promise? A threat? Did it matter? She had given them her answer already.

She lay awake for a long time and stared at the cement ceiling. Salty, unshed tears ran down the back of her throat, draining away like her dreams. A real degree, embed races, moot surgery: all gone. Hope receded to an unreachable distance in the hours after midnight.

The restless murmurs and snuffles of slumbering bodies surrounded her. She had to get herself out of the shelter, but how? Sleep took her at last, before she could come up with a good answer.

———

The morning bell rang. Grey daylight filtered in through high, small windows. The room came to life with yawns and groans and the creak of metal frames. Marmeg left the shelter after eating breakfast. She needed fresh air.

Last night's rain had left the city smelling earthy and clean. She walked to a dilapidated park bench and sat down to check her messages.

She had a new one from T'shawn: MINERVA RACE COMM SAY RULES BE RULES. FANS BE FIGHTING BACK. His earlier message – the one he'd sent at the start of the race – caught her attention: GIVE ME YOUR GEAR IF YOU TOAST OUT?

He'd meant it as a joke, but she *had* almost toasted out. The words nagged at her mind. Her gear: exos, chips, sleeves. They would be worth something. She felt sick at the thought, but she couldn't conceive of a better solution. The shelter would give her two weeks. After that, she'd be out on the street with no address. Her ratings would plummet. No one would employ her. The sooner she could get back home, the better.

MEET UP AT ELEVEN-OH? she sent to T'shawn. He responded that he could.

She spent the morning answering what passed for fan mail, not that she had any prior experience to go by. Half of it was hateful – the usual rants against unlicensed and postnatals freeloading off taxpayers – and the other half exhorted her to fight Minerva. DON'T LET THEM DENY YOU! BE THE HERO WE NEED! But in her heart, she couldn't be what they wanted, not with this race. Not until she won by her own means.

The walk to T'shawn's place took ten times longer than it would have with functional calf muscles. She limped past cars for hire that she couldn't afford. Her mind jittered with lingering frustration, and her whole body ached, but her mood lifted when she entered the abandoned building where her friend lived and worked.

He was holed up in a back room, well hidden from the street by small, paper-covered windows. Black-market gear gleamed in stacks around the perimeter. A workbench sat against the far wall. An oscilloscope, multimeters, probes, and screens littered its surface.

T'shawn gave her a rueful smile, grasped her shoulder in a half hug.

'Win some, lose some,' he said.

'Full right, that.'

'What you be here for today? Twice in a week is a special treat.' He flashed his toothy grin at her.

'Want a quiet talk for a sell-back.'

His grin vanished. 'Marm, you not serious. What you do with yourself if you go back to nat? Don't let this race bull get you lost in the head, friend.'

'Only way out, brud,' Marmeg said. 'Get good credit for all my chips. Pay out school fees. Do the slow way.'

'Old way, more like,' he said, grimacing.

'Yeah, well, Ma kicked me out. Stuck myself good.'

'Not again!'

Marmeg pressed the case with the two unused chips into T'shawn's hand.

'How much for these plus the seven inside? Three of 'em busted.'

T'shawn sucked on his upper lip as he typed in some numbers. He showed her the final tally on his screen.

'Minus a few hundred for the surgeon.'

It would be enough to cover the first tuition instalment for the elder care programme – enough to get her back into

Amihan's good graces.

'Trigger it. Set me up with the doc. Got any work for me?'

'Naw, Marm, nothing paid. Barely cover my own. Get me some new code, might get you some treats again.'

'Can't test code without chips.'

'Don't give up, hear? You one of the best we ever got, and you need to get out. Show the kids what can do. Get me a benefits gig someday.'

Marmeg laughed to cover the lump in her throat. 'Stay sane, brud. Ping me when you got the date.'

———

Her next stop was a used-gear shop. She'd filched many of her own exos from the trash cans in the back. The owner didn't mind, since he couldn't fix the broken stuff, and he would buy some of Marmeg's flips when she found an upgrade. The inside of the store was crammed with floor-to-ceiling shelves. Dusty plastic bins brimmed with parts sorted by function.

Marmeg walked along the scuffed, dirty floor tiles and went straight to the front counter. Chips gleamed inside the glass case. She put her bag of gear down, fighting the urge to curse at the tiny capsules. The sound of clanking metal drew the owner from the back. His tight grey curls contrasted with his dark skin, and his face crinkled into a broad smile.

'Marmeg! What can I do for you?'

She marvelled that he remembered her name. She couldn't recall his. He'd tolerated her filching, but he hadn't been this friendly in the past.

'Want to sell this.'

'Sure, sure. You must be in line for some real gear now.' He sorted through the items, putting the torn and bloody sleeve straight into the trash, separating the older-generation parts from the new.

'No more gear. I'm out.'

'But the race – you can't be quitting now?'

So, he knew about that. 'Full busted. Race took the last of it, and Mom kicked me out. Need money.'

He pushed the gear aside and leaned on the counter. 'Well that's a shame, considering your skills. I thought a scout would've picked you up by now, got you some sponsors.'

She shook her head.

'Have you seen your ratings? The news today? You're up. Minerva's sinking like a rock.'

Marmeg shrugged. Ratings had their value, but they didn't pay for tuition or put food on the table.

The shop owner sighed. 'This stuff isn't worth much. How about a job? You fix broken gear for me, I pay you by the hour. And you have to work here, in the front, and record some ads for the store. Help me boost my ratings.'

A job would let her save up, get Felix his license. Maybe earn back her chips if she kept at it long enough. *What for?* she thought. *You'll never race again. They won't let you.* Regardless, she could use the money for any number of things, not the least of which was keeping Amihan off her back.

'Okay. Deal. Gotta sort some other business. Start next week?'

'I'll see you on Monday.'

As Marmeg exited the shop, her cuff zapped her wrist. T'shawn had a surgery scheduled for her the following day.

———

Marmeg sat at a plastic table and ate a basket of hot, greasy fries with the last of Jer's credit. It was a treat to herself. Her legs and arms ached from the chip extractions, and pain pills were the only thing saving her from a stunning nitrous-oxide headache. She'd kept the chip in her brain stem. The surgeon wanted extra fees for that, and T'shawn had talked his buyer into a better price overall. It made little difference to keep it.

She traced the table's random cracks and stains with her left pinky. The heat from the fries soothed her raw throat. She'd managed to save her tears until she was alone. When she had let them loose, the sobs had ripped through her like an angry spirit. She needed the comfort of starch and fat.

Her cuff buzzed, and Marmeg looked down to see a stranger requesting a live call. The face belonged to an older man with lined brown skin, dark eyes, and wire-rimmed glasses. A full beard and moustache matched his salt-and-pepper hair. She accepted the call.

'Miss Guinto, yes? I'm sorry to bother you like this. My name is Sachiv Jagadisha.'

Marmeg stared at him blankly. The name sounded familiar, but she couldn't recall why.

'I'm Ardha's father,' he explained. 'I'm calling you because I discovered that not only do we need to thank you for helping our child, we need to apologize for zir behaviour. Ardha was gravely injured, and zie has been unconscious until today. They can't save zir natural legs, but zie is lucky to have so many enhancements already. They say they can integrate artificial muscle and bone into what's left.'

Marmeg nodded, unsure how to respond. At least now she knew why the name and face were familiar. She could see the family resemblance.

'I'm sorry. I'm talking on and on. My child became lucid only yesterday. Zie confessed to my wife – zir mother – what zie had done to you earlier in the race. And yet you were kind enough to save zir at the cost of the race itself. You are truly selfless, and you have been very badly rewarded. My family and my colleagues who supported Ardha in the race – we would like to extend a credit to you.'

'Can't take it.'

'Please, you must. It's not a great deal of credit, but we feel badly about what our child has done.'

Marmeg forced herself to speak in slow, full sentences. 'Can't take it, sir, but thank you.' She took a deep breath and decided she might as well tell him the whole truth; a confession for a confession. 'I didn't win the race fairly. Got help from some...mountain people who took me to shortcuts. One of them brought me to Ardha, else I never would've found zir. And then –' She broke off, looked away from the kind brown eyes on the screen, and lapsed into familiar rhythms. 'Did what was right. Tried to make up for cheats, you know?'

Ardha's father sighed. 'You were sabotaged and you were aided, but that was the work of others. It is you who saved our child. Forget the race and think of the credit as a token of our gratitude. Please. My wife will not forgive me if I accept your refusal.'

Marmeg's face flushed with suppressed tears. *Don't be an idiot. This money can only help, and why shouldn't you get something for all that you went through?* But the thought didn't sit right. A different idea nibbled around the edges of her mind.

'You got any pay gigs?'

'Sorry?'

'Paid work. A job I could do,' Marmeg clarified. 'Got a college admit but can't pay for it. That's partly why I raced. Want to get an embed design degree. Get myself out of this hole. Make a better life, you know? I can code for you.'

'I see.'

Sachiv's expression was distant, and Marmeg wondered if she'd blown her chance. Her school contests were too far in the past to count, but she had her own designs, the illegal ones.

'Custom built the 'ware for my own rig.' She pulled her screen from her cargo pocket and sent him the source code. 'Take a look. Steady pay beats a credit dump, you catch me?'

Sachiv smiled at her. 'Quite right. Yes, quite right. Unfortunately, we cannot hire you until you have at least the bachelor's degree. Let me think about it some more. Perhaps I can find a happy solution. I'll get back to you.'

The call ended. Marmeg leaned back against the hard curve of the seat. She looked around at an unfamiliar world, noise buzzing around her. Her heart raced and her hands shook as she took a bite of the fries. They were cold. She couldn't care. Her fate stood poised on a pinnacle, its balance as precarious as her footing during the race. Which way would it land?

Marmeg dumped the unappetizing food in the compost bin and walked outside. A hot, dry breeze whispered through her hair as she strolled along the uneven cement sidewalk and waited for the call. And walked. And waited some more. Sweat itched on the back of her neck. The afternoon wore on and the sun beat down from a cloudless sky, but sitting still proved impossible.

She was gulping water from a tepid public fountain when her cuff zapped. The message came from Ardha's father, all text: NO JOB OFFER. SORRY! BUT WE CAN PAY TUITION AND IF YOU KEEP UP YOUR GRADES, YOU'LL HAVE A REMOTE INTERNSHIP OFFER FOR NEXT SUMMER.

Marmeg didn't know whether to laugh or cry, so she sat on the sidewalk and did both. Getting a fully paid college education was monumental. Even her mother couldn't deny that. She could save all her money from the job at the used gear shop. Get her chips back. Get Felix's license. Race again next summer. She could go home.

She sent a reply to Ardha's dad with an electronic signature and the address to her empty credit account. Marmeg's mind reeled as she limped her way back to the shelter to collect her bag. In a few weeks, she'd be a college freshman, surrounded by hordes of licensed, well-groomed kids who took for granted three meals and a bed and hot showers. Life was about to get real different.

A half-dead pine tree grew in the empty lot to her left. She recalled the scent of alpine air and melting snowflakes, of cold stone tunnels and wet earth, and she hatched a plan: for another year, another race. She would win on her own merits. Trap the Mountain Mikes into revealing their hand. But, most of all, she wanted to dance like the wind over granite mountaintops.

ACKNOWLEDGEMENTS

This book encompases about four years of work, which means a lot of thanks are due, but the bulk of them is to the Codex Writers' Group. Their inspiration and support saw me through the period that produced the majority of this work.

A huge thanks also to the support of my family as I balanced my time as an engineer, parent and writer. Many of these stories were written in the gaps I carved out of my day – late at night, on weekends, on planes or trains or in cars. Thank you for your patience and encouragement.

Thanks also to my cadre of beta readers, especially when I needed feedback on short notice.

And last but not least, I'm deeply grateful to all the editors and publishers who first brought these stories to the world and nurtured them into the forms they take today.

PUBLICATION HISTORY OF THE STORIES
IN THIS VOLUME

'Loss of Signal' was first published on Tor.com in August 2018.

'Contingency Plans for the Apocalypse' was first published in *Uncanny Magazine* in January 2018.

'Microbiota and the Masses: A Love Story' was first published on Tor.com in January 2017.

'An Unexpected Boon' was first published in *Apex Magazine* in November 2017.

'Nava' was first published in *Gamut* in January 2017.

'Binaries' was first published in *Lightspeed Magazine* in June 2016.

'The Egg' was first published in *Nature Futures* in March 2015.

'The Boy Who Made Flowers' was first published in *Mothership Zeta* in July 2016.

'Ships in the Night' was first published in *Daily Science Fiction* in May 2015.

'Gaps of Joy, and a Knot for Love' was first published in *PodCastle* in October 2016.

'Strange Attractors' was first published in *Daily Science Fiction* in June 2014.

'Soft We Wake' was first published in *Analog Science Fiction and Fact* in January 2019.

'Runtime' was first published by Tor.com Publishing in May 2016.